A LOVE TO HEAL HER HEART

AMISH BROTHERS

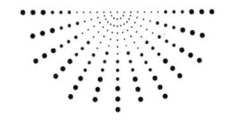

SARAH MILLER

SWEETBOOKHUB.COM

FIVE AMISH BROTHERS

Welcome to the first of 5 books about 5 Amish brothers.

Like most families, our brothers love each other. They are also, very different people, with different hopes and dreams. When they lose their daed, and the harsh reality of their future is revealed can they pull together to find love and a secure future, or will it pull them apart?

Join them and the residents of Faith's Creek as they grow into men their daed would be proud of.

Blessings,

Sarah Miller

Join my newsletter for accessional free content and to be the first to find out about new books.

CHAPTER ONE

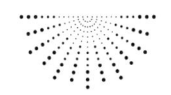

A hacking cough jerked Jeremiah Phillips from his sleep. Part of him wanted to walk from the room, close his eyes in his own bed and sleep for a week but he would not do that.

Filled with guilt and sorrow he reached for a glass of water. "*Daed*, how are you?"

Helping his *daed*, Henry to sit, he guided the water to his lips. Henry fought down the cough to take a sip and as Jeremiah pulled the glass away he noted the swirl of blood that sank to the bottom.

"Drink again, it will help." Jeremiah held his *daed's* frail shoulders and guided the glass to his lips. The cough was deep and hacking and shook the old man's body to the very bones.

Eventually, the coughing stopped and Jeremiah lowered Henry to the bed and handed him a handkerchief.

"I'm *gut*," Henry said. "Do not worry son, for soon, I will walk in paradise with your *mamm*." A smile crossed Henry's face. The first one Jeremiah had seen in a long while.

"Don't talk, *Daed*, you need to gain your strength."

"Help me sit up. I hear my Maria calling to me, I do not think I have long."

The sound of his *mamm's* name brought hot tears to Jeremiah's eyes. He missed her so much and the realization that soon, his *daed* would be gone too felt like too heavy a burden. Of course, it shouldn't be. He was the eldest at 29 and had been looking after the farm for 8 months now. It was only when he took over that he realized what a sorry state their finances were in. It was another burden that he shouldered alone, not wanting his brothers to know how bad things were.

"I should fetch my brothers."

"*Nee*, not now. Help me up."

Jeremiah lifted his *daed* and packed pillows behind him before lowering him gently back. At one time Henry had been a strong vibrant man but now he was just skin and bone. The lung disease had taken from him his very essence and Jeremiah knew that it was time for him to join *Gott*. He knew this was right for Henry, but selfishly he didn't want to let his *daed* go.

"Now, I want you to listen to me," Henry said. "I have much to tell you and little time." A fit of coughing stole Henry's breath and fresh blood was sprayed into the white of the handkerchief.

"Rest, we can talk tomorrow," Jeremiah said as a tear slid down his cheek to drop onto the blue patterned quilt that his *mamm* had made.

"*Nee*, your *mamm* is waiting and though she tried, she was never that patient." A smile crossed Henry's face and he glanced into the distance. "I can't wait to be with her. It hurts, my boy, but there are things I have to say." The coughing started again.

Jeremiah handed over the glass of water and could see strength in his *daed's* hazel eyes. Strength and a clarity that had not been there for some weeks.

"Go on," Jeremiah said and held his breath so that he could hear every word.

"You know by now that the farm is mortgaged. I know that you and my sons, all my sons, can bring it back to profit and that it can support all of you. Promise me that you will not let foolish pride get in the way of asking for help!" Henry looked deep into Jeremiah's eyes.

"I promise, *Daed*." Though he did not know what he could do, what help he could get he knew he would try.

"You have your *mamm's* blue eyes. They remind me so much of her and I miss her dearly."

"You will see her soon, *Daed*." Jeremiah swallowed the lump in his throat and bit down hard to stop the tears from falling.

"There are other things I want to see done. I will look down on you all with pride," Henry said. "These things I want you to promise me that you will do. Will you honor my last wishes?"

Jeremiah took his *daed's* bony hand in his and squeezed it gently, willing that his love could travel through that contact. The skin felt like paper dried and old and he feared that if he squeezed too hard it would crack away and break the brittle bones. "I will do anything for you, *Daed*, anything."

"That is *gut*, you were always stronger than you knew. I think I kept you under my mantle too long. I should have let you flourish more."

"*Nee*, do not say that. I have loved my life and loved learning from you."

Henry coughed once more and the pain was clear on his face. His hand did not have the strength to raise the handkerchief. Jeremiah took it and mopped the blood from his lips.

"I should have listened to you more, should have encouraged you more. It was not my own *daed's* way. He was very strict, I tried not to be like him but I think I followed in his footsteps..."

"*Nee*, you have been a great *daed*, I could not ask for more."

Henry chuckled. "You make an old man very happy. I want you and ALL my sons to know that I am proud of them."

"All," Jeremiah said the word without thinking.

"*Jah*, all. I want my family back together."

"I will do my best." Jeremiah swallowed again and wondered if he could achieve such a feat... if he even wanted to.

"The next thing I want for you all, is love. You cannot understand joy until you have felt the love I have felt for my Maria. It is the most wonderful thing to go through life with a *gut* and loving woman at your side. It makes everything so much easier, so much better, it brings you closer to *Gott's* love and fills life with joy."

Once more coughing stopped the words and Jeremiah leaned over and held his father, giving him support to lean into while the cough subsided. Once it stopped the flickering of the oil lamp cast a pallid glow on a skin so white it was almost translucent.

"Why not rest now and we can discuss this tomorrow," Jeremiah said.

"*Nee*, there is *nee* tomorrow for me. Listen, son, for this is important."

Jeremiah nodded for he did not trust his voice and once more bit down on his lip to stop the tears.

"I know that your brothers will resist. You must let them know that I go to my grave in peace knowing that you and they will honor my wishes. The farm will be made *gut,* they will all find a *fraa* or you will arrange *gut* marriages, and the family will be back together and in peace. Can you do that?"

"I can, for you, *Daed,* I can do anything."

Henry squeezed onto Jeremiah's hand. "Marriage can be hard, it takes faith and work but when you allow love in, it wins and it sustains you. I want you all to have that joy."

"*Jah, Daed*, I understand. Now rest and let me call Dr. Yoder. He will give you a tonic or maybe it is time to go to the Englisher hospital."

"*Nee*, never. Dr. Yoder has said that there is nothing medicine can do for me. Now, it is down to faith and I have faith and love in my heart. Do not fear what is to come for it is glorious and I am ready. I wish to die in my home, with my family, covered in the quilt that Maria made me. What better way to go than wrapped in her love? Promise you will do as I ask, promise me you will trust in *Gott.*"

Jeremiah squeezed his *daed's* hand and nodded as tears ran from his face and dripped onto that hand. "I will, *Daed,* I will."

"Troubles will come your way. I wish I could, but I can't prevent that, but you will get through them if you trust in *Gott*. Can you do that?"

"*Jah*, I will, always."

"Now, I am in pain but that is not to be feared. Sometimes we are birthed in pain but that is nothing to fear, sometimes we pass over in pain, this is nothing to fear either."

"*Daed*, I have to help."

"Mop my brow, offer me water, and pray with me. That is all the help I need."

Jeremiah began to pray. Over the next hour, the coughing got worse and worse and he called for his brothers. Abraham was sleeping in the next room. "Send for Dr. Yoder and call our brothers."

Abraham walked to the bed and kissed Henry's forehead before leaving to harness a buggy.

Jeremiah held his *daed's* hand and mopped his brow as the pain got worse and then it was as if it all stopped.

"Maria," Henry said and there was a smile on his face. He was reaching his hand out toward the bottom of the bed. "It is so *gut* to see you, my love." Henry chuckled and the peace that came over his face was remarkable and a joy to see.

Jeremiah stared at the corner of the room where Henry was looking, he could not see anything but he knew his *daed* could.

"You came, my love, my Maria," Henry said and his hand moved back onto his chest. His eyes closed and he released his last breath.

"Take care of him, Dear Lord, Amen." Jeremiah wiped the sweat from his *daed's* brow and the blood from his lips. He held his other hand until his brothers arrived, or at least 3 of them. Bringing Colin home might not be so easy. It didn't matter, he had made a promise and he would do as his *daed* asked.

CHAPTER TWO

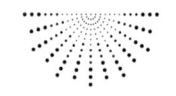

Jeremiah watched the last breath leave Henry's body. It was both a peaceful moment and one filled with anguish. What would he do now? How would he cope? How would he fulfill his last wishes?

As the tears streamed down his face he hugged his father close and hoped that he could stand tall beneath this burden. He had to hold the family together, to bring it back together, and to see it thrive, but he wondered if he was up to the burden.

What could he say to his brothers?

The sound of footsteps on the stairs brought him back to the present. He lifted his head and dried his eyes. It was time to be strong and to put his trust in faith. "Dear *Gott*, guide my words tonight and see my *daed* safely in the arms of my *mamm*, take care of them, amen."

The door burst open and Moses, the youngest Phillips brother at just 18 burst into the room. Seeing the still form of their father he dropped to his knees and let out a wail. "You should have called us earlier."

Jeremiah swallowed as he looked into a reflection of his own face. The kindly-looking boy was bereft and ran a hand through his tousled brown hair. Jeremiah saw his own blue eyes staring back at him, accusing him. "I'm sorry. It happened quick and he didn't want me to leave. I didn't know it would be now."

Uri was the next through the door, with his red hair and tears in his green eyes he always looked a little different to the brothers and Jeremiah knew he felt it at times. At 20 he was closest to Moses. "When did he leave us?"

"It was just a moment ago," Jeremiah said.

Uri went around the bed and dropped to his knees. He took Henry's hand and Jeremiah almost told him to leave it. The way his *daed* had reacted it was as if Maria had placed that hand there. But it didn't matter now, for both of them had left.

Abraham came into the room with Dr. Yoder. There was a pain in his icy blue eyes and a touch of fear. "Are we too late?"

"I'm sorry, boys, but he is gone," Dr. Yoder said. "You go make some coffee and I will take care of things for now."

No one moved. Jeremiah felt as if he was frozen in fear. How could he get his brothers to follow him, to agree to their *daed's* wishes, how could he keep the family together if he couldn't even make his legs move?

"Go now, boys, Henry is in a better place and you need to make preparations."

Jeremiah felt his legs move and he walked to the door. "Come, *Daed* spoke to me before he passed, there is much to talk about."

Slowly, they climbed down the stairs and almost automatically, Jeremiah put a poker in the stove and put on coffee to boil. He sat at the table and his brothers joined him.

"What can we do?" Uri asked.

"Tonight we talk about him and *mamm* and all the *gut* memories. Tomorrow I will speak to Bishop Amos Beiler and the undertaker, we will bury him and we will do as he wished."

"Why is it you he told?" Abraham asked.

He was the brother that was always alone, the one who questioned things, the one who thought he was an outcast. Jeremiah knew it would be hard to get him to understand if things went badly wrong. They often butted heads and Abraham needed time for himself. He had even been known to go away for a few days to think.

"I was just there," Jeremiah reached out a hand to his brother but Abraham pulled it away and stood.

For a moment it looked like Abraham would leave but instead, he poured them all a coffee and slumped back down at the table.

"What did he say?" Abraham asked.

Jeremiah swallowed a lump in his throat but it refused to go down and he couldn't seem to get the words out. Only he and Henry had known how bad the farm was doing. He had hoped to turn the situation around before the brothers needed to know but he knew that he had to tell them.

"Talk to us," Uri said, blinking back the tears.

"First of all, he told me how proud he was of all of us." Jeremiah smiled through his own tears as he remembered the words and the look of pride on Henry's face.

"That is *gut*," Uri said.

"Not all of us." Abraham took a sip of his coffee and put it down on the table with a bang.

Jeremiah did not think that Abraham had meant to be so aggressive with the mug and he looked at the spill of coffee on the oak table. This was just anger and a feeling of being out of control, he knew that, for he felt it too.

"He did say all, and he wanted us to bring Colin back."

Murmurs and protests went around the table.

Jeremiah raised a hand. "That is a conversation for another day. I made a promise and I will do my best to keep it. For now, I want to tell you about the most amazing thing that happened.

The room fell silent and the three brothers all looked at Jeremiah. Once more, the pressure seemed too much for him to bear, he had to break their hearts telling them they might lose the farm and their home, but not tonight. Tonight they would talk.

"What happened?" Uri asked.

"*Daed* was in pain and he knew he was going. He had been coughing for some time and the look in his eyes was not *gut*. Despite this, he told me that we are born in pain and sometimes we die in it. He told me he had nothing to fear."

"I don't want to hear of him dying in pain," Moses said. "I don't want to think of that as his last memory."

"Take my hand." Jeremiah held out his hands and for a moment his brothers just looked at him. Then they all joined hands. "Something happened. Suddenly, a look of peace came over *Daed's* face and he was talking to *Mamm*. He reached out his hand and the light of the Lord filled his eyes.

"He said that she had come for him and that he was happy to leave and then he was gone and at peace. It was the most amazing thing I've ever seen."

Abraham pulled his hand out of Jeremiah's "You're just saying this to make us feel better, it doesn't!"

A cough from behind them had them turning to the doorway. Dr. Yoder was standing there. "Do not discount this. I have witnessed the very same thing many times. A loved one came to guide Henry over. To be with him and to remove his fear. To show him love for the next part of his journey. We are people of *Gott*, you should believe in His miracles."

CHAPTER THREE

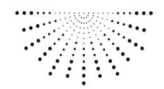

*E*ster Harley looked around the small and neat living room that she shared with her Aunt Rhonda. With a smile, she lay down the quilt she was working on and wiggled her toes next to the fire.

It had almost burnt down to embers and she knew she would have to fetch some more wood soon, but she was comfortable and didn't want to wake her aunt. The room was bathed in shadow as there was only one lamp burning over her shoulder, it was just enough to allow her to work.

Aunt Rhonda had not been well today and Ester feared that she was not long for this world. Dr. Yoder had told them that the Englischer hospital would keep Rhonda going longer but her aunt would not hear of leaving her home.

"I'm happy here," she would say. "Happy and content, I've had a *gut* life and you have been a treasure."

Ester stood and took the quilt her aunt was working on from her lap. The oil lamp had almost gone out and it cast shadows as she moved. Folding the quilt, she lay it on the table next to her own. It was nice to while away the evenings talking and quilting. But as she looked down at the fine work she wondered if her own fingers would be able to quilt once Aunt Rhonda was gone. An emptiness seemed to fill her with cold and she wondered if she would ever touch a quilt again. Could she do it alone, without the company and joy that Aunt Rhonda brought?

A lock of blonde hair fell from her *kapp* and Ester pushed it back. For a moment she was afraid of the future. How would she cope once her aunt had gone? It was her only reason for living and she dreaded to think of the lonely days to come.

"Do not look so sad, my little love," Aunt Rhonda's voice was weak but the smile on her face was genuine.

"*Ack*, I'm sorry, Aunt. I just wish I could make you better."

"*Nee*, there is a time for all things and this is the end of mine. I am happy, my only worry is you."

"I will be fine, you raised me well and I have the district around me. Bishop Amos and Sarah Beiler will see that I want for nothing. You should worry about yourself."

"I know you will be, but you have sacrificed so much for me. I wish you at least had a friend."

Ester swallowed and forced a smile on her face. "I have sacrificed nothing, you gave me love. I have Leah, she is a *gut* friend."

"But you should have more, a male friend, I wish you would get married."

"*Ack*, you know me. I'm awkward with other people and too shy to connect. Do not worry, I will be fine."

"I want you to know that I have prayed on the matter," Aunt Rhonda said.

Ester came to her side and dropped to her knees taking Aunt Rhonda's hand as a fear clasped onto her heart. There was something in the way Aunt Rhonda was speaking, in the rasp of her breath that terrified her. It couldn't happen now, it was too soon.

"I believe that you will find a friend soon. You must be open to it and pray for it. You must give people the chance to see that big heart of yours and promise me you will be happy."

Ester nodded and lowered her head to hide her tears.

"Promise me."

Ester swallowed the lump in her throat but still, she couldn't speak. She swallowed again and raised her head. "I promise, for you."

"Then, I go in peace, *denke* for everything." Aunt Rhonda let out a few breaths and her eyes closed. She slumped back in the chair and her hand in Ester's was limp. She had gone.

Ester let the tears fall as she prayed for Aunt Rhonda's soul. Prayed that life would be easy, prayed that she could keep her promise and yet she knew it would be hard. Whenever she was with people she got tongue-tied and that made her nervous. When she was nervous she snapped and came over as unfriendly. It was not what she intended but it always seemed to happen.

People said she bristled like an old porcupine and no matter how much she tried, it always ended up the same. "Please, *Gott*, let it be different this time. Let me get it right for Aunt Rhonda."

* * *

The following morning Ester harnessed Ned, her buggy horse, and set off to see Bishop Beiler. Her eyes were still red and she had hardly slept. Her *kapp* and dress were wrinkled, she knew she should have changed but knew that Amos and Sarah would understand.

It was almost like she was drawn to them, pulled to the loving comfort of their arms. It had seemed wrong to leave Aunt Rhonda alone but she knew she had to go.

When she arrived at the bishop's house she knew he wasn't there. The shutters were drawn and the normal warmth that came with the house was missing. Pulling the buggy over she called to a man walking along the road. "Where is Bishop Beiler?" Why had her words sounded so abrupt?

The man raised his head and took off his black felt hat. His light brown hair was tousled from it and a touch of annoyance crossed his light blue eyes. "He's away in Ohio visiting."

Ester recognized the man as one of the Phillips brothers. She didn't think it was the one who used to tease her for stuttering but she wasn't sure. A flush of anger went through her. She needed the bishop, what could she do now?

"I'm Jeremiah Phillips, can I help at all?"

"You help?" the words were spoken harshly but not out of anger, out of desperation. "I... I need Amos... my aunt... she's dead."

"Oh, I am so sorry. I just came back from seeing Bishop Victor Marshall, would you like me to come with you, or to help at all?"

Ester felt her jaw fall open. She knew that Bishop Marshall was a *gut* man but she didn't find him quite as comforting as Amos." When will Amos be back?"

"Not in time," Jeremiah said.

"Oh, *denke*." With that, she geed the horse into movement not wanting this man who may have teased her to see her crying.

"If you need help come see me," he shouted after her.

Ester knew that the Phillips family were the last people she needed help from but as she drove away, she realized she had been very rude and she felt awful. Already, she had let Aunt Rhonda down.

CHAPTER FOUR

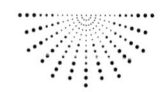

*E*ster did not know how she got through the meeting with Bishop Victor Marshall. The man had only been made a bishop this year and he did not have the grace that Amos seemed to exude. His *fraa* had passed and his home was sterile and devoid of refreshments.

"There are to be two funerals on the same day," Victor said. "Henry Phillips also passed last night."

Ester raised her head, that was why the Phillips brother had been to see the bishop. She had been so rude to him. "Oh, of course, I'm sorry to hear about Henry. I presume they will be conducted together."

"*Nee*, that will not be suitable. I will conduct Henry's first and then Rhonda's later that day."

"But... but... people will not be able to attend both. If you do that my aunt will not get the..." Ester's words froze in her throat. If she had said that her aunt would not get the respect and sendoff she deserved it would be frowned upon. This was a tribute to *Gott*, not to Aunt Rhonda.

"That is the best I can do." Victor folded his arms and looked annoyed.

Ester wanted to shout at him and this time it was not because she was shy. It felt as if she was letting her aunt down both with the funeral arrangements and with her promise to mix more. Why was everything so hard?

"Of course, Bishop. I will go and prepare Aunt Rhonda for viewing."

"*Gut*, I will have the word spread, will you need help?"

Ester knew she should say *jah*, it would be hard work alone and it was an opportunity to bond with someone but she couldn't. She had to do this herself, had to let her own grief out in private before she could welcome the district into her home." "*Denke*, but I will be fine."

"Well, you know where I am if you need me, *gut* day."

Ester had been dismissed, she felt her knees wobble as she stood but she raised her chin and walked out of there with as much hope as she could muster.

"Trust in *Gott*," she heard the words in Aunt Rhonda's voice in her head but as she was driving away she saw the Phillips buggy driving to the bishop's house.

Had the Phillips put pressure on the Bishop to push her aunt's funeral out? They had to have or the funerals would be together. A touch of anger set seed in her belly and as she drove home she could feel it laying down roots.

* * *

Ester did not know how she got through the next 3 days. At first, she prepared her aunt's body, cleaning it and dressing her in her wedding gown. Aunt Rhonda had always been a trim woman and was frail now so the plain blue dress fit perfectly.

The following day the district began to pay their respects. Ester was awkward, and short with most of them and regretted it each time the people left.

"*Gut* day," Albert and Mary King said as they entered the house. "We are sorry that Rhonda has gone."

"*Jah*," Ester said and stood there, not inviting them in. She seemed to have frozen on the spot and her tongue was thick and unruly in her mouth. "It is *gut* of you to call."

"Of course, we call, girl. Which way?" Albert asked. His face showed that he was not impressed.

Ester swallowed and tried to talk. "I... I... in the I... I..." Shaking her head, Ester pointed to the door to the living room."

Albert walked past her mumbling.

"Do not worry about him," Mary said. "He hates these things. How are you?"

"I'm okay." Ester managed and hoped that these would be the last callers today. Her poor nerves could not take much more.

"It has been a bad week with Rhonda and Henry. May *Gott's* blessing be with you." Mary squeezed Ester's hands as she walked past.

This was how the visits went. Ester said the wrong thing or could say nothing. The house was full of food that had been given but she was not hungry. Well, she could serve it for the meal after the funeral. Surely, it would be well attended?

The days were exhausting and she wondered how she would get through them. Sipping at a coffee she heard the first friendly voice since Aunt Rhonda had died.

"I'm so sorry, Ester," Leah Chandler called as she came into the house. "I was away visiting my brother. When the news reached me, I came straight back."

"That is fine."

"*Nee*, it isn't. I know how hard you would find it to cope." Leah poured herself a coffee and took a seat at the table. She took Ester's hands in hers.

A great sense of relief came over Ester. She had not let Aunt Rhonda down for she already had a friend. Leah, like her, had been a bit of an outcast. Leah was born with very pale skin and violet eyes. Dr. Yoder had said that it was a lack of pigmentation and nothing to worry about. That she should just be careful in the sun. That *Gott* made us all unique, and that it should be celebrated.

Some of the *kinner* at school had taken to teasing Leah because of her skin and eyes and Ester because of her stutter. The two girls had stuck up for each other and developed a friendship. Though Ester was still awkward, with Leah it was not bad and she enjoyed her company.

"I have been so busy that I hardly noticed." Ester shrugged for she knew that Leah would understand the little lie.

"I'm here now. What is this about the funerals being separate?"

Ester raised her hands dropping Leah's back to the table with a thud. "Bishop Marshall told me when I informed him of Aunt Rhonda's death. I believe that the Phillips brothers had already seen him. Maybe they wanted Henry to get…" Ester stopped, surely, Jeramiah Phillips would not do this, but what other reason could there be?

"Colin was always the mean one. I'm so glad he left the district on his *rumspringa* and didn't come back. I don't know why the other brothers would do this but you must be right. I will talk to them… without them what will you do about the quilts?"

Ester felt another blow to her future. It was like a punch in her guts and it took her breath away. The thought of quilting without Aunt Rhonda filled her with dread but she had not even given her income a second thought. Now she realized that Henry Phillips had sent customers their way, and now he was gone, her business would dry up. What could she do? "I don't know."

"We will pray on it." Leah took her hand and they prayed.

In her prayers, Ester asked for the strength to get through the next few days in a way that would honor Aunt Rhonda. She asked for calm and a *gut* turn out to the funeral. However, she knew that she had been frosty to those who had visited the house to view her aunt. Given the choice, they would spend the afternoon at the Phillips house, not hers. *What had she done?*

"Amen," Leah said.

"Amen," Ester parroted, though she knew her prayer had been a litany of self-pity.

"Leave this to me. I will talk to the Phillips and let them know how mean I think they have been."

Ester smiled. It was *gut* to have someone in her corner and to see her small friend so full of fire gave her hope.

"*Denke*, but there is no need. Would you quilt with me some nights?"

"*Jah*, I would love to."

Ester smiled. She had a friend, someone to quilt with. Now all she needed was to get through the funeral tomorrow and find a way to sell her quilts. It was doable, wasn't it?

CHAPTER FIVE

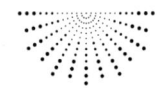

*E*ster followed the funeral buggy in her own and was despondent at the small turnout. There were a mere 20 buggies in the procession. The rest of the district would be at the Phillips house.

When they arrived at the graveyard she reached for Leah's hand.

"Do not worry," Leah said. "This is all just a mix-up." There was a touch of red on Leah's cheeks; Ester knew her friend was angry.

Bishop Victor Marshall talked about Rhonda and the promise of *Gott* as the few people who attended filed past Rhonda's coffin one more time. It was a plain oak box with no handles or lining as was the tradition.

Rhonda looked at peace, and that was all Ester could think about. Though she knew that this was the start of a new part of her life it was hard to let her go.

The coffin was lowered into the hand-dug hole and the few people there sang Jesus my Shepherd and then Walking with *Gott*. Then it was over and people were drifting away.

"Please call in later," Leah said as Ester mopped at her tears, but she doubted that people would.

Bishop Marshall came over. The man's grey hair and beard seemed to have a life of their own and Ester had the urge to straighten his hair but she kept her hands to herself.

"This is *Gott's* will," he said. "Call me if you need me, I have to visit the Phillips farm now." With that, he turned and walked away.

Ester let out a gasp and dropped to her knees. Whether the bishop didn't hear or didn't care she didn't know but he did not turn back.

Leah helped her to her feet. "He is as deaf as a post, or so they say." She smiled and guided Ester back to the buggy. "Let's take you home."

"*Nee*, what is the point? No one will come."

"You do not know that," Leah said as she helped Ester climb into the buggy and took Ned's reins."

Ester looked at her. "What have I done?"

"Do not think this, people don't take the time to know you."

Ester tried to smile but she knew what to do. "I did not visit Henry, that was wrong of me. I just couldn't face it. I knew I would say the wrong thing. Let's go see them now."

"Are you sure? I am angry at the Phillips, you must be livid."

Ester nodded. She was sure, but she wasn't sure what she would say or do. What they had done was mean, they could have shared the service and the meeting after. That would have been the Amish thing to do, the *gut* thing to do and she couldn't understand why they had felt it necessary to push her out."

* * *

Leah drove to the Phillips farm and pulled Ned alongside the other buggies. The two women unhitched the buggy and tilted it on its end, taking Ned to the paddock prepared for the horses.

"Maybe, we should have left him hitched?" Ester said. She didn't want to stay that long.

"*Nee*, it would look wrong."

"*Jah*, you are right." Ester wondered if she would ever get the hang of talking to people, of being with them.

"Relax," Leah said.

They were greeted by Abraham and Uri. "I'm so sorry for your own loss," Uri said but his icy eyes seemed to see right through her.

"And I yours," she replied as Leah led her in.

Bishop Victor Marshal had a plate of food in his hand and was laughing with a group of men. This angered Ester, even though she knew it was not an insult to the dead. Death was a part of life and this gathering was a time to discuss the deceased, to speak of the *gut* times, and to remember their contributions.

To one side, Ester noticed that Jeremiah was standing alone. Just seeing him there filled her with anger and she rushed over with Leah at her side.

* * *

Jeremiah just wanted everyone to leave. He felt as if his face was aching with smiling and greeting people and he left his brothers to it for a while. It was time for him to be alone. It was just 3 days since Henry's death, but already the bank had asked for a plan. He had no idea how to make one and no idea how to tell his brothers just how deeply they were in debt.

Closing his eyes he prayed for a sign, for help, for anything that could keep his family afloat and on the land that they had worked for so long.

"How could you?" Ester said as she came up to Jeremiah.

Jeremiah opened his eyes and lifted his head to see Ester Harley's angry face. "How could I?" he asked.

"How could you do this to my aunt?" Ester raised her fists and shook them. The grief she had held back was desperate to surface.

"I don't know what you mean."

"Stop this," Moses Phillips hurried over.

Jeremiah could see that people were starting to stare. He could hear mumblings about Ester and what did she expect.

Leah stepped in between Moses and Ester. "It was wrong to move Rhonda's funeral."

Moses stopped in his tracks. "You are the ones who are wrong, you are spoiling things. We are here to celebrate my *daed*, please go."

"It is all right, Moses," Jeremiah said. "Walk with me." He held his hand out in front of Ester and nodded for her to lead.

Ester was so angry. Once more she had done the wrong thing and she felt tears flood her eyes. Wanting to escape she walked in the direction she was pointed.

Once they had rounded the barn Jeremiah stopped and turned to her. He could see the hurt on her face and he understood it. Like him, she had lost her rock and like him, all the responsibility going forward was on her.

Though he did not approve of her behavior he understood it and knew that Henry would too. Henry had often said that Ester was misunderstood. That she was a fine woman with much potential.

"I'm sorry about Rhonda," he said. "I was going to call over to your house later to pay my respects."

"But why did you insist that the funerals were separate?" Ester asked.

"I didn't. The two deaths coming so close was something I could do nothing about and I didn't ask for special treatment, I didn't even know that they wouldn't be together until we arrived at the graveyard."

"Then why did this happen?" Ester held her hands up before him and realized that everyone was staring at her. That Abraham and Uri were rushing over. What had she done?

"What is going on here?" Bishop Marshal asked.

Ester looked at him and at Jeremiah. "I wondered why Aunt Rhonda had been pushed aside by the district that she supported for so long."

A series of gasps went up from the people watching and then the denials began.

"I'm sorry," Jeremiah said. "This was not our intention."

Ester looked into his eyes and they looked genuine. Had she misread things so badly? "Sorry," she said, and grabbing her dress, she turned to run.

CHAPTER SIX

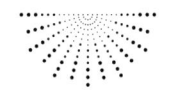

"What is wrong with that woman?" Moses asked.

"She's grieving." Jeremiah felt awful. Already he had let Henry down for he knew his *daed* would not be pleased with such an outcome.

There was mumbling of discontent, some were understanding of Ester but others were saying that she reaped what she sowed.

"Please, let us respect all the dead," Jeremiah said as he stared into the faces of his neighbors for the first time without his *daed's* support. "Let us treat this day with respect and understand that grief affects us all differently. I did not know that Rhonda's funeral would be separate. I did not want that and I want us all to respect each other."

Mumblings of *jah* went around the crowd and people drifted away.

"It is fine, she is best to mourn alone," Moses said.

"*Nee*, I will call on her soon. We have behaved badly and *Daed* would not be proud." Jeremiah put a hand on his youngest brother's shoulder and squeezed. He could see the pain deep in Moses's eyes. The boy was not angry with Ester, as such, but angry at everything.

Jeremiah turned to the bishop and nodded for him to walk. Once more he made his way to a more secluded part of the property. "Can I ask why you did separate the two funerals?" Jeremiah asked.

Victor shrugged his shoulders. "I thought it would be better. That it would be too much to do them together. I think I was wrong."

"*Jah*, you were, but I understand. Amos will be back soon."

Victor looked a little embarrassed. "I hope I haven't disappointed him too much."

"Amos will see the *gut* in you and in Ester. He will make this right. Do not worry."

Victor nodded and walked back to mingle with the crowd.

Jeremiah closed his eyes for a moment and steeled himself. He could get through today, and tomorrow he would make a plan. He didn't know how but he would pray on it and trust that *Gott* would help.

Opening his eyes he rounded the barn to see his three brothers waiting for him.

"Do not worry about Ester," Abraham said. "You know how she is."

"Abraham is right," Uri said. "She upsets everyone with her rude ways. I don't know how *Daed* put up with her."

"Because her quilts and Rhonda's sold," Moses said with a smile.

The three siblings were on the same page. They thought that it was best to push Ester aside but Jeremiah felt he couldn't. There had been something both brave and vulnerable about her behavior and he knew that they had contributed to her pain. That was not a *gut* thing to do, not something he could let go of.

"*Jah*, I think she is probably grieving and terrified of what is to come. She has lost her aunt, the person she spends the most time with, the person she has selflessly looked after for years. She has also lost *Daed*, a man who respected her and who provided her with her main source of income. I will visit her tomorrow and see how we can help."

"What?" Moses said.

"*Nee*," Uri added.

"Let her be!" Abraham turned and walked away.

The thing was that he couldn't and he wouldn't. Somehow he felt that Ester was in the same predicament as they were and it felt right to help her. Of course, he didn't even know how to help his own family, so how would he help her?

CHAPTER SEVEN

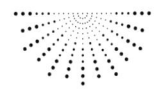

Ester burst through her door and kicked off her shoes. She very rarely wore them and had only done so today in a hope that it was the right thing to do. She had been wrong, there were few women wearing shoes and it had made her feel even more of an outcast.

Why had she attacked the Phillips brothers? If What Jeremiah said was true, then he had done nothing to deserve it. Dropping to the floor she let her tears come. *What had she done? What could she do to make it right?*

The tears were still falling when she heard the sound of a horse and she realized that she had left Ned at the Phillips. Wiping at her face she pulled herself to her feet. It took a gargantuan effort, for she had lost all her energy when she lost her aunt.

Taking a breath, she made her way to the door to see Leah climbing out of the buggy.

A flush of love went through her. Leah had stuck by her, had not abandoned her, that must be a sign of hope. "*Denke, Gott* for my friend."

Leah ran across the ground between her and pulled Ester into her arms. "Let it all out," she said as she rubbed her back.

"I'm so sorry," Ester sobbed against her friend's shoulder.

"It is fine. You have always been there for me. Come, let's put Ned away and get you some food. When was the last time you ate?"

For a moment, Ester couldn't remember, but she had hardly touched a thing since she lost Aunt Rhonda, that was three days ago and would soon be four. Ester shrugged as she unhitched the harness and led Ned to the stable.

It didn't take them long to rub him down and give him a feed before turning him into the paddock behind the house. The horse kicked up his heels and then rolled in the grass before wandering away to graze beneath the shade of a sugar maple tree.

"Now some food." Leah led the way to the house and checked in the cool room. She pulled out an Amish casserole that was filled with sausage, eggs, and cheese. While it was warming in the stove, she made coffee and then served everything up at the table.

"I must apologize to the Phillips, will you help me draft a letter?" Ester said as she picked at the food. The casserole was surprisingly good and she was suddenly ravenous but still couldn't seem to force herself to eat. It was a strange feeling. It was as if her body wanted life to go on, but her mind wanted to give in.

"I can, but I do not think you need to worry; forget this and put it behind you for now."

"I know that Aunt Rhonda would not be happy with how I behaved. I have to apologize."

Leah shrugged. "The thing is, emotions are running high at the moment and I feel that it could make things worse."

"Then I will just send a note saying I am sorry. Then I will keep away."

"You need sleep," Leah said. "Tomorrow we can talk about it."

Ester realized that she was exhausted and she nodded. Leah insisted on doing the dishes and that she would stay in the guest room. She also sent Ester up to bed.

Despite how she was feeling, Ester fell almost instantly asleep. She said a quick prayer of *denke* for Aunt Rhonda and asked for *Gott's* guidance and then she crawled beneath her blankets and was asleep almost as soon as her head hit the pillow.

Ester woke in a cold sweat. She had been dreaming of Aunt Rhonda and of Jeremiah. Both of them were angry with her and told her that she must leave. It seemed like a sign and she knew she wouldn't sleep again tonight. Quietly and quickly she dressed and made her way downstairs.

Lighting a single candle she pulled pen and paper from the bureau and began to write.

To the Phillips brothers,

Please forgive me for my terrible behavior today and please accept my deepest condolences on the death of Henry. He treated me well, and I should not have done what I did. I have no excuses, and can only blame it on lack of sleep and grief.

I will not trouble you again and hope you can forgive me.

Ester Harley

She folded the note and straightened her *kapp*. It was still dark out, but the walk would do her *gut* and she wanted this note to be there for when the brothers awoke.

The ground was cold to her feet. The seasons were already starting to turn and without the sun's rays, it was invigorating to feel the chill beneath her soles.

Ester walked quickly for she could see a faint glow on the horizon. The brothers were farmers and they may rise early. The last thing she wanted was to meet one of them. Though she felt a little like a thief in the night, she knew that this was the way it had to be.

As she placed the note in the mailbox she saw a light come on in one of the upstairs rooms. Had she disturbed them or were they simply rising?

It didn't matter, she had to go. She turned and ran from the house hoping that this was the end of it and praying that she would find another way to sell her quilts.

CHAPTER EIGHT

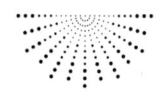

Jeremiah made coffee and walked to the mailbox. The flag was up from yesterday but he had been reluctant to check. The last thing he wanted, was another letter from the bank, but he knew it was time to face the music, so to speak.

There were two letters. The first was from the bank, demanding that he come in to talk about clearing the debt or that they would foreclose on the farm.

Pain, like a knife, stabbed at his temple. So far he hadn't thought of what he could do. So far he hadn't spoken to his brothers about the problems. It seemed more urgent to bury Henry and mourn, but he knew that he had to do something... the problem was... what?

The next letter was a simple note. As he opened it he felt more pain. The last thing he needed to deal with was Ester Harley. Opening the letter he read and a deep sense of shame came over him.

To the Phillips brothers,

Please forgive me for my terrible behavior today and please accept my deepest condolences on the death of Henry. He treated me well, and I should not have done what I did. I have no excuses, and can only blame it on lack of sleep and grief.

I will not trouble you again and hope you can forgive me.

Ester Harley

How had he become so bitter? *Daed* would not be pleased for Ester was suffering, probably worse than he was, for she was so alone. The note touched him deeply, for he knew the courage it had taken to write and deliver it. Would he have the courage to apologize in such circumstances?

Trust in Gott. The words were in *Daed's* voice and Jeremiah closed his eyes. With the letter beneath his clenched hands he prayed.

"Dear Gott, guide me to Your path. Lead me to provide for my brothers. Give me patience and faith and let me help Ester in a way that would make *Daed* proud."

He prayed silently for faith and guidance, for a plan for the farm and for Ester, and in his mind's eye, he saw a board on the highway pointing to the farm offering genuine Amish quilts and produce. Could it be so simple?

Excited, he knew he had to tell Ester about it today. Later, he would call on her, and later, he would talk to his brothers. He would explain how bad things were and tell them that together they could make it work.

For now, he went to the barn and pulled out an old piece of wood. It was large enough so he cut it and sanded it, painting it white. Once it was dry he would paint on an advertisement and he felt sure that their luck was about to change. They could get through this.

* * *

Ester and Leah sat on the porch quilting. It was warm today, but the season would soon turn.

Ester was working on the quilt that Aunt Rhonda had not finished and from time to time she had to blink back her tears.

"That is so beautiful," Leah said. "She had such skill."

"*Jah*, much better than mine."

"*Nee*, you are every bit as *gut* at quilting, she taught you well."

Ester smiled, that was a compliment she could take. "I guess she did. What am I to do with these?"

"Why don't I talk to the Phillips brothers? I can see if you can still sell the quilts to them."

Ester shook her head. "*Nee*, after what I did I don't think so."

"We all make mistakes, it is the Amish thing to forgive and to help. Service to others is our highest calling; give them the chance to experience that." Leah smiled.

"You were always so clever, but I don't know. When Amos gets back, maybe he can help me. Or maybe I could find a shop in Bird-In-Hand to sell my quilts, others do that, don't they?"

"Maybe, but don't shut this door when it may still lead to your salvation."

Was that what she was doing? Was she letting her pride or her fear push people away once more? Aunt Rhonda would not be pleased. Maybe she should go and see the Phillips brothers, maybe she should try.

A sigh escaped her, the thought of doing so filled her with fear. When she was afraid she snapped and became tongue-tied. How would such behavior ingratiate the brothers to her? *Nee*, they had enough troubles of their own; she must find her own way.

"I have to go, I am at work soon," Leah said. "Come see me if you need me."

"*Denke* for everything, I will."

As Ester watched Leah go, she decided to take a walk and talk to *Gott*. It was the way she felt closest to Him, walking in nature with her feet on the ground and just asking for a sign or talking. It would make her feel better and maybe it would lead her to her path.

CHAPTER NINE

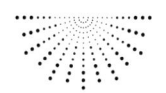

The grass was warm beneath Ester's feet. The sun was shining and warmed her face. Closing her eyes, she followed the path along the creek and let her senses open, listening to the gentle flow of the water. The birds sang in the trees and the leaves whispered as she passed. This was what she liked to do sometimes. Leah would laugh at her, saying you will fall, you will stumble and hurt yourself, but Ester never did. Whether it was because she had done it since she was a *kinner*, or whether it was because He was guiding her she did not know.

What she did know, was that she felt blessed, walking this way. Blessed, guided, and loved.

To her left, she could hear voices and she opened her eyes and looked. She had walked to the edge of the Phillips farm and the brothers were working in the field. The brothers were picking strawberries for the market and in the field next to them the tomatoes were also ready for harvest.

Ester felt fear run through her. Had they read the letter? Were they still angry with her? She would not blame them. Turning, she began to retrace her footsteps and retreat back to the safety of her remote house.

Her house, this was the first time she had thought of it as such and she felt ashamed. "I have not forgotten you," she said.

"Forgotten me?"

Ester turned to see Jeremiah smiling at her.

"Sorry, I... I..." Dropping her head she tried to force the words to come out and to stop the heat that was coloring her cheeks. "I was talking to Aunt Rhonda." Ester looked up to see understanding in Jeremiah's light blue eyes.

"I wanted to say *denke* for your apology. It was not necessary, but it was appreciated."

The silence dragged between them. Ester tried to think of something to say but couldn't so she shrugged and went to walk on.

"Wait," he called. "I want to speak to you. I had an idea that could help both of us… if you will listen. It came to me after my prayers this morning."

Ester turned back to him. Was this the sign she had been looking for?"

"Don't even try," Moses said coming up behind them. "She can't even be decent enough to talk to you."

Ester felt anger and hurt boil up inside of her and she turned to flee.

Jeremiah grabbed her arm and she was pulled up short. She turned to him, anger pinking her cheeks. He let go.

"I'm sorry, I didn't mean to hurt you." He turned to Moses. "Go back to the house. If you cannot be civil to a fellow human in pain then I do not wish to see you."

A look of shock and shame crossed Moses's face. "I apologize, Ester." He took off his hat and clutched it in front of him before turning and going back to the house.

Jeremiah turned back to Ester. There was something about the look on his face that made her want to trust him. Maybe he could be her friend? Maybe, this could be her way of honoring Aunt Rhonda and of making a living for herself. "I will hear you out," she said and realized that once more the words had come out harsher than she meant them.

Waving her hands in frustration she tried again. "Sorry, I am not *gut* with people. I get nervous and my words come out so abrupt."

"I understand. I will take that into account, but you had no problem talking to Henry; think of me as him."

Ester swallowed. He was right, she had always been able to talk to Henry, why was that? "I think it was because he respected me."

"I respect you. The whole district does. We all know how well you cared for Rhonda and that service makes you one of the best of us."

Ester felt herself smile. No one had ever spoken to her like that. "*Denke,*" she managed. "Your idea?"

"Amish quilts are highly sought after. I was hoping to put an advert on the road about the quilts and our produce to bring people to the farm. If you will let me sell them from there, maybe I could sell our produce at the same time."

"I... I don't know, they are my quilts and take a lot of work." She wanted to say that she could not afford to give him any of the proceeds but the words wouldn't come out and so she shrugged and walked away.

"Just think about it. I would not expect anything from you, this would be a way to help us both. Maybe you could help us and we help you?"

"I know nothing of farming," Ester called without looking back. She wanted to run. The thought of letting go of her quilts was too much. She knew of Wanda Lapp who had handed her quilts over to a market holder and had been left with nothing. The man had been a fraud, and had taken them, and then denied that they had ever met.

"Please think about it," Jeremiah called before he turned back to the fields to continue picking the strawberries. He just hoped that they would not have to make them all into jelly or feed them to the pigs. So far, sales had been poor and the fruit would not last long.

Ester walked along wiping at her tears. Why was she so afraid? Why couldn't she take a chance?

"Ester, stop."

Ester turned to see the youngest of the Phillips brothers, the one with the red hair, running after her. Panic clawed at her chest.

"I did not mean to frighten you. I'm Uri and I wanted to talk to you."

Ester nodded.

"I think our farm is in trouble. Jeremiah is not a bad man, trust him and give his plan a chance."

"I don't know, it is risky for me."

"Pray on it, that is all I ask." He smiled.

For a moment she was able to smile back. She could see a little of Henry in all the brothers and it was comforting. "I will, and I am sorry about Henry."

"*Jah*, we will miss him, Rhonda, too. For them, we should be *gut* friends and neighbors. As such, we should help each other."

Ester nodded. The words touched her deeply. "I will pray on it," she said before turning to walk home.

* * *

Uri walked back to Jeremiah and Abraham. "I tried."

"You knew she was never going to be easy to work with. Why are you wasting time on her when we have so much to do?" Abraham laughed and walked away.

Uri raised his hands and shook his head.

"There are things I have to tell you. We will talk tonight, but for now, I have an idea. Ester is part of that and I believe it is what is meant to be." Jeremiah squeezed his brother's shoulder. "Continue with this, I will be back shortly."

With that, Jeremiah went to the barn. He had finished painting the sign and it looked wonderful. A strawberry, tomatoes, eggs, and quilts decorated it along with the words Genuine Amish Quilts and Produce. An arrow pointed to the farm gate.

It took him just 30 minutes to mount the sign on the edge of their land close to the road, he prayed he was doing the right thing and prayed that he could make this work. His family depended on him and on this.

CHAPTER TEN

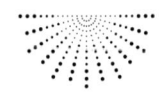

Jeremiah was waiting for his brothers when they came down to breakfast. He had already collected the eggs and some strawberries. He had checked in *Daed's* store and found 3 quilts that had not sold.

After doing this he had taken an old cart and added a roof to it. He had propped it up and painted it placing a sign on the front, Genuine Amish Produce.

Part of him felt wrong doing this but he knew that *Daed* would be proud of him, he felt it and felt more relaxed than he had since his *daed* had passed.

After breakfast, the cart would be dry and he could start and load the produce onto it and hope that people would come.

"Morning," Uri said as he came down the stairs. "Is there coffee? I will have a quick sip before I do the chickens."

"*Jah*, coffee is on the stove. I already did the hens, I was up early."

"*Ack*, you need your rest."

"There are things I have to tell you all. Are your brothers up yet?"

Uri smiled. "They are, they should be down soon. Moses was moaning about early morning again, he is always so grumpy in the morning."

Jeremiah chuckled. The rest of the family were naturally early risers but Moses had always struggled. "Maybe we can get the farm to a place where he can have a lie in."

"*Ack, nee*, you would never get him out of bed."

Jeremiah chuckled as he cooked some eggs and served them with bacon just as the two other brothers came down the stairs. Abraham looked bright and ready for the day, Moses's hair stood on end and his eyes were hardly open.

"Sit, eat," Jeremiah said as he served breakfast and put the coffee pot on the table. He was used to this routine, though in fairness his brothers took their turn.

Breakfast was muted, everyone was still grieving and also, Jeremiah knew that his brothers knew something was wrong. Henry had kept the worst of the news from them but they could sense it. The lack of customers was hard to hide.

At one time, they had a thriving business with people driving miles for their produce, they also had an arrangement with a market stall. It meant they could make *gut* money in the season and survive the rest of the year.

Moses was the last to finish. He pushed his plate away and stood to clear them from the table. "What are we doing today?" he asked.

It was a silly question. They had all farmed the land all their lives and knew that the season dictated what they did. It was time to harvest and sell, of course, yesterday's crop had not sold. Neither had the days before or the one before that. There was a big tub of strawberries that would be rotten if they were not used soon.

"First, I need to tell you some things," Jeremiah said.

"Are you going to tell us how you are going to change things?" There was a challenge in Abraham's eyes.

"That is not what I said." Jeremiah took a breath and closed his eyes for just a moment. He asked for guidance and strength. Opening his eyes he smiled at his brothers. "We are family and we need to stick together."

"*Ack*, then where is Colin?" Abraham asked.

"Stop this," Uri said. "Let him talk."

Abraham muttered but poured himself another coffee and nodded.

"Before he died, *Daed* asked me to look after you all…"

"Really, we are not *bopplis*," Abraham said.

"Then stop behaving like one." Uri gave his brother a stern look.

"Bringing Colin back into the family was one of the things *Daed* asked me to do," Jeremiah said. "There is bad news too, you all suspect it, and I'm sorry to confirm your fears…"

"Is the farm bankrupt?" Moses asked before he could finish.

* * *

Ester spent time quilting and worrying about the house and how she would cope. Her outgoings were small for the house was owned and she grew a few vegetables. Maybe, she could swap some mending, or a quilt, for some chickens and meat. But who would help her?

Leah came around most days and sometimes stayed for the night, but she had her own life. Each day and each night, Ester prayed over Jeremiah's proposal, but no one came to see her. There was no sign telling her that this was her path. She was starting to feel abandoned.

It was late afternoon and she decided to walk along the river, the famous Faith's Creek. This time, she turned in the opposite direction to the Phillips farm. As she was walking, she wondered if she was resisting *Gott*. If she was fighting Him in her wish to stay alone. It was silly, childish almost but was that what she was doing?

Maybe, the fact that no one came was telling her that she had to help herself. Maybe it was telling her that she had been offered help and that she should take it. Why was she so stubborn?

Maybe she should go and talk to Jeremiah one more time. After all, what did she have to lose?

CHAPTER ELEVEN

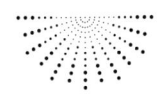

*J*eremiah had managed to explain to his brothers that they were not quite bankrupt. He didn't explain how close they were, he then told them of his plan and of the board on the road.

"How will that help?" Abraham asked.

"I'm hoping that it will bring people to the farm, while they are here they will buy our goods."

"This is silly, we simply need to work harder," Moses said.

"Working hard when nothing sells is not going to help. What about all the fruit that is spoiling?" Uri asked.

"I have plans for that. I'm going to make it into jelly and bottle it and sell it too."

"This will not work," Abraham said but before he could say anything else they heard the sound of a car pulling up outside. "What is that?"

Jeremiah took a breath and prayed. "Let's hope it is a customer. Help me carry this out." He pointed to boxes full of strawberries, tomatoes, cucumbers, lettuce, and the three quilts.

"You've been busy," Moses said and jumped up grabbing a couple of boxes and his hat. He raced out of the house.

Jeremiah followed him to see a lady with brown hair and wearing a smart skirt suit looking a little lost. He prayed that she had not just called in for directions.

"*Gut*, good morning," he called. "Apologies, we are a little behind this morning and are just setting up."

"That is no problem. "I'm looking for a genuine Amish quilt. What do you have?"

Jeremiah felt a little disappointed. These quilts would not last long.

Uri stepped forward with a big grin on his face. "They are very popular, we only have three left and they will not be here long."

It looked like he was a natural salesman.

"Let me see."

Uri beckoned for her to follow him and he placed the box with the produce down first arranging it before he set the quilts down.

"These are beautiful." The woman turned them over, inspecting each one. "How much?"

Jeremiah stepped forward, he was about to say $400 which was what they had sold for in the past.

"These two are $1000 and this one is $1200," Uri said.

Jeremiah felt his heart tumble. Uri had just lost them… well, Ester… a sale.

"That is a good price," she said. "They are worth every penny. I can give you $400 cash for the $1200 quilt; will you take a check for the rest?"

"Of course."

"I will have these too," she said picking out 3 punnets of strawberries and some vegetables.

The rest of the morning they had a steady stream of customers. The quilts sold out before they took a break for coffee. After that, a few of the customers were angry that there were none left. Uri quickly made up a sign to say quilts sold out, for now, more coming soon, check back often.

Despite the lack of quilts, they sold more produce than they had in months.

While they had a break for coffee they talked.

"We have to get more quilts," Uri said. "I love doing this, it is such fun."

"*Jah*, I'm sure we can find someone to make us quilts. If we pay them we can keep more of the profits," Abraham said.

"I want to talk to Ester first," Jeremiah said. "I think *Daed* would have wanted that."

"*Daed* left us in trouble, we need to look after ourselves." Abraham had taken the knowledge that they were broke hard.

"Let's see what we can arrange with Ester first," Jeremiah said. "We can always have more quilts if they sell in large enough numbers."

Abraham shook his head. "You are useless. You couldn't persuade this woman to work with us. What hope do you have of making the farm work?

"I will keep my faith and do my best. Together we can do this."

"Colin would do a much better job," Abraham said before he turned and walked out.

"I will talk to him," Moses said as he followed his brother back to the fields. The sound of a car horn had Uri jumping up from the table. "Customers." The grin on his face was infections.

Once his brother was gone, Jeremiah went back to dehulling the strawberries. He had never made Jelly, but how hard could it be?

As Jeremiah leaned over the sink he saw Ester walking up to the farm. Even from this distance, he could see she was angry. It was clear in her posture and the touch of red on her cheeks. Why had he not told her what he had done?

CHAPTER TWELVE

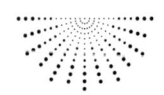

Jeremiah walked to the door to see Ester staring at Uri. What could he do? She was clenching her fists and getting ready to say something. Uri was simply grinning at her which wouldn't help.

"Ester," he called. "I have just made coffee, join me."

Ester turned and looked at him and seemed to wobble on the spot. She was obviously trying to make a decision.

"It is *gut*, and I'm sure Henry and Rhonda would want us to stay as friends. I have something for you too."

Ester nodded and walked up to him.

"Come, sit." He pointed at the table and poured her a cup of coffee. The room was a mess and he had to move some strawberries out of the way.

"I have $3200 for you from the sale of the last quilts that you left here," Jeremiah said and noticed how her jaw fell open.

"You sold all 3, for how much?"

"$3200, well, some of it is in a check. Sorry about that, we were not very organized."

"How many were there again?" Ester's eyes were wide and her mouth still hung open. She was really very pretty.

"Three, it seems that Uri is a born salesman. He said that they sell for that in other places so we should ask the same."

"I didn't agree to this," Ester said. "I was outside for a while, I heard you shouting."

"I'm sorry…" For a moment he didn't know what to say. It was inexcusable that she had heard them fighting but then again families had disagreements, it was part of being a family. Suddenly, he felt as if he knew what he was doing. "Brothers, unfortunately, we fight at times.

Each of us is still tired and hurt, and there are a few problems with the farm that my *daed* had kept from us."

"I understand," she said, "it is hard to run a business when all your time is spent caring for another. I think most of the district knows that you are struggling."

"They do?" This surprised him but it shouldn't have. Theirs was a close community and he realized at that moment what *Daed* had meant when he spoke of pride. The district would help them. They would buy their produce and work in the fields if needed. All he had to do was let them know. He also realized that Ester might not be capable of asking for help and he was determined to give it.

Now, all he had to do was work out a way that they could help each other, one that she would accept.

Uri popped his head around the door. "We sold out of eggs. I'm going to see if there are any more and then fetch some more strawberries from the fields. Listen for cars?"

"I should go," Ester said.

"Please, *Daed* would have wanted us to work together. Will you allow me to sell your quilts?"

"I will think about it. Now, what are you doing here?" Ester looked at the mess in the kitchen.

Uri let out a sigh. "I'm sorry. We have a lot of almost spoiled fruit. I was going to make Jelly."

"Do you know how?"

Jeremiah shook his head.

Ester laughed. It changed her face completely and made her look so beautiful that he felt a tingle in his chest.

"Then let me show you."

As Ester rolled up her sleeves and began to order the kitchen, Jeremiah whispered a prayer of gratitude.

CHAPTER THIRTEEN

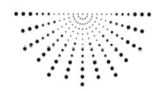

Ester had spent all night thinking about the proposal that Jeremiah made to her. She was intrigued and she knew that it could benefit both of them. She also knew that Aunt Rhonda would have approved but something was holding her back. She just didn't know what. Was it fear of being taken for granted? This happened but the Phillips had never been like that. Was it fear of getting involved with the brothers? Fear that she would not cope? This was something new and her instinct was to stay away but that was not what Aunt Rhonda wanted for her.

Thoughts tumbled and turned in her mind keeping her awake, but still, she had no answer.

She had prayed on it, had spoken to Leah and she had heard that Bishop Beiler was back. This morning she would speak to him and see what he would say. It was on her mind to visit the bishop but she knew he would be busy and she kept putting it off.

Closing her eyes she sat at the table and sipped at a cold coffee when there was a knock at the door.

Ester started and jumped knocking the coffee over and letting out a mutter of anguish.

The door opened and Amos and Sarah Beiler walked in.

"Goodness, child," Sarah said and rushed over. She put a cake on the side and grabbed a cloth to help clear up.

While she did this Amos put the kettle on the stove and began to make coffee.

Ester sank back into her chair and let the tears fall. Sarah put her arms around her and held her close. "I'm so sorry we were away. Do not worry, we are here now, for anything you need."

Soon they were sipping hot coffee and eating the delicious coconut cake. Ester wanted to ask about the funeral but she was scared that she would say the wrong thing and drive these *gut* people away.

"I heard what Bishop Marshal did," Amos said. "Do not blame him, it was a lack of confidence that had him make the wrong decision."

"What?" Ester asked.

"He did not feel confident enough to do both services at once."

Ester knew her mouth was open but she couldn't seem to close it. "I blamed Jeremiah Phillips. I am so horrid, no wonder no one likes me."

Sarah was holding her in her arms again and Ester felt comforted.

"That is not true," Sarah said. "We understand you and many admire you. I spoke to Rhonda about this and you just need to get out more. You can do it now, you have the time."

Ester wondered if that was true, could she get out more, could she make friends? For a moment, her heart leaped, was there even the possibility of love in her future?

*　*　*

After Amos and Sarah had left, Ester felt that she had been given her sign. It was time to trust, time to move forward, and time to see if she could work with Jeremiah. Why did she only think of him? Surely, she would be working with all the brothers, and yet, in her mind, she could think of only Jeremiah.

For the next hour, she sorted through the house and pulled out all the quilts that had been made and never sold. There were a few she could not bear to let go of but many were already ready for sale.

There were also a number of table cloths, napkins, crib blankets, and other items that would sell for a lower price. Once they were loaded into the buggy Ester froze. She had intended to drive them over to the Phillips farm and accept Jeremiah's proposal. Now, however, she felt unable to climb into the buggy.

Fear rooted her to the spot. What if she said the wrong thing? What if he changed his mind? What if people wouldn't buy? What if they worked with someone else?

Ned pawed the ground with his hoof and nickered, he was impatient and wanted to be moving.

"It looks like I need a bit of your courage," she said and stroked the horse beneath his forelock.

Ned leaned against her and nibbled at her apron looking for a piece of carrot that she kept there for him.

"Ok, here you go." She fed him the carrot, patted his neck, and climbed into the buggy. There was only one way to find out if this could work and that was to do it. As she steered Ned out of the drive she felt as if Aunt Rhonda approved. All she had to do was behave as Aunt Rhonda would want her to. How hard could that be?

The drive was just a few minutes and as she pulled near to the Phillips farm she saw the sign advertising produce and quilts. Panic flared in her chest. Had she lost out? Had they already partnered with someone else?

Driving past she steered the buggy down to the farm.

"Morning," Uri called. "It is a lovely day."

"*Jah.*" Ester pointed back at the sign, that was just visible, unable to say anything.

"It is *gut*, isn't it? Jeremiah made it and it is bringing lots of customers."

Ester felt her throat close and she didn't know what to say. Should she be angry that they had put the sign up without asking her... or at least, telling her?

"Are those more quilts for me?" Uri asked and his smile was infectious as he bounded over to the buggy. He patted Ned's neck and offered her a hand.

Ester was not sure what to do or how to react. People so rarely interacted with her that she just wanted to turn Ned around and drive away.

"Morning," Jeremiah called, as he carried punnets of strawberries from the house as well as a box of the jelly that she had helped him make. "The coffee is on, leave Ned to Uri, and come and share a cup."

Uri walked to him and took the boxes. Jeremiah came over to the buggy and offered his hand.

Ester took it and as their fingers touched, she felt a tingle race up her arm. It was a strange sensation, a little shocking, but not unpleasant. What was going on?

CHAPTER FOURTEEN

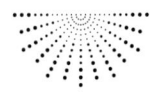

*E*ster clung to her coffee. Jeremiah was sitting across the table from her and had explained everything again. She was to provide quilts, they would sell them, and she would keep all the money for them.

It seemed to *gut* to be true. "Do you not want anything for selling them?"

Jeremiah smiled and there was something about it that made her stomach flutter. A frown came over her face and she could see he was worried. She was doing things wrong again and closed her eyes wishing that Aunt Rhonda was here. Aunt Rhonda always took care of these things.

"*Nee*, we don't need to take anything from you. I don't think Henry did."

"*Nee*, he didn't… as far as I know." She shrugged her shoulders and managed a smile. "But, he passed the quilts to someone else." Ester had to admit she knew very little about the transactions. She had always planned to find out, but there always seemed so much time. It felt wrong to talk of things that would happen after Aunt Rhonda's passing, it felt like it would make it happen sooner. Of course, one's time was in *Gott's* hands and there was never as much of it as you hoped.

"Then do we have a deal?" Jeremiah held out his hand for her to shake.

Ester hesitated. The coffee cup was something she could cling onto and she felt reluctant to let it go. However, he was waiting for her and so she nodded. Reaching out she shook his hand. Just the brush of his fingers sent tingles up her arm and she drew her hand away a little too quickly.

"You have made me very happy," Jeremiah said. "I know that Henry would have wanted this."

The smile on his face was warm and genuine but Ester was filled with panic and emotions she did not know how to handle. "I am happy to go along with this... but it does not make us friends."

The look of disappointment that crossed his face hurt her. Why had she said that? Where had the words come from? Sometimes she thought that she said the wrong things just to fill the silence. It was silly and she had to learn to change.

An apology was lodged in her throat but before she could swallow the lump that was blocking its path he nodded.

"I can live with that. It may take time for you to trust me, but I hope that you will learn to do so. I want us to be friends and I see no reason why we can't be. When will you have more stock to sell?"

Ester let out a sigh of relief. "I have brought all that I had available. I'm working on two more quilts now, they will be ready by the end of the week."

"That is wonderful."

Jeremiah smiled and once more she felt a tingle in her stomach, what was happening?

"I want you to know that we are here if you need anything," Jeremiah said. "We are business partners and neighbors. *Daed* warned me that I should not let my pride stand in my way. It is not easy, sometimes it is hard to ask for help, but if you need anything, please ask."

"*Denke*, I will."

They spent the next hour discussing how to move the business forward. The increase in customers was helping but, so far, it was not enough.

"Why don't you have an event?" Ester asked.

Jeremiah shrugged. "What do you mean?"

"Well..." What had she meant? Closing her eyes she thought for a moment. It came to her. "Do you remember the Mullet farm, many years ago?"

Jeremiah shook his head.

Now she was worried, she would insult him and this would all be over.

"Be bold," the words were Aunt Rhonda's.

Ester swallowed. "I do not wish to insult you. I'm not *gut* with words. The Mullet's farm was having trouble. A day was arranged when people came to the farm to buy Amish produce. Lots of people from the district donated something small. They helped set up stalls and man them on the day and they provided food and coffees for the customers. It was a great success and if I remember, the farm became so well known that they had no problems after this."

Jeremiah was thinking. "Could we do this?"

"*Jah*, of course... you could." Ester hoped that she was not giving him false hope. Would people help? How would they get the word out? There was so much she did not know."

"I think it is a great idea, but how?"

Ester smiled, it felt *gut* that he was uncertain too. He had always seemed so bold, so confident and she realized that he struggled just like she did. Somehow, that made her feel better, more confident, and determined to help him. "Perhaps we should follow Henry's advice and bite down on our pride. I could talk to Amos and see if he could help." Why had she said that? Why didn't she let him do this without her?

"That is wonderful. I would like that very much."

Ester smiled. "We would need to set a date, maybe give a few months for people to prepare?"

The look on Jeremiah's face said it all, a few months was too late. She had not realized just how much trouble they were in.

"*Jah*, of course," Jeremiah said, quickly hiding his disappointment.

"*Nee*, I think we can do this much quicker. I just thought about the seasons. We are at the height of the soft fruit season, so it would be best to do this soon. I will talk to Amos today or tomorrow and I will speak to you soon."

Before she could lose her courage she drank the last of her coffee and almost ran from the house.

"*Denke*," Jeremiah said as he helped her into the buggy.

There it was again, that strange tingling feeling that leaped from his fingers up her arm and into her heart. As she took hold of the reins, she wondered what she was doing. She had committed to speaking to the bishop and if this event went ahead, she would have to speak to a lot of people. Would they help her, would she be able to do it?

Fear traced a finger down her spine and she wished that she had stayed well away from the Phillips farm. All she had done was give herself strife.

CHAPTER FIFTEEN

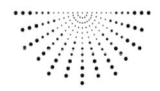

*E*ster spent the rest of the morning picking up her quilt and putting it down again. Sometimes, she stared at it for long minutes, but so far she had done hardly a stitch. There was an ache in her stomach, a sickness that rose in her throat every time she thought of what she had done. Why had she offered to help?

Throwing the quilt down again, she stood and walked to the door. She would take a walk and she would pray. Turning away from the Phillips farm she walked along the creek side. The grass was refreshing to her feet and the breeze played with her *kapp*, threatening to tug it from her head.

Closing her eyes, she stopped and sank to the ground. Sitting there, she let her fingers run over the blades of grass, feeling the moisture within them and she let out a sigh.

"Dear *Gott*, help me. I do not know what to do."

Then she let her fears and her worries pour out of her. Handing it all over to *Gott* and asking Him what she should do. It seemed to take forever, and once she was finished she felt fatigued. Lying back, she kept her eyes closed and drifted off to sleep.

Since she had lost Aunt Rhonda, sleep had not been easy and she was exhausted. Out here, in the fresh air, she fell instantly asleep and woke a short while later.

Sitting up, she straightened her *kapp* and apron and let out a sigh. Though she had only slept for 20 minutes she felt refreshed and she knew what she had to do. She would ask for help and she would do the best that she could. No one could ask for more.

Feeling much more optimistic, she made the walk to the Beilers' house. Amos and Sarah would help, she was sure of it. However, as she got closer she started to worry. What if they were busy? They had only just come back and more important people than she would be in need of their help. As she reached their garden, her feet froze and she wanted to turn and run.

"*Gut* day, Ester," Bishop Beiler said.

Ester jumped for she had not seen him weeding in his garden. There was a small fence and he had been bent down behind it. Her hand flew to her chest and her mouth dropped open with a gasp.

"*Ack*, I'm so sorry," Amos said, standing up a little awkwardly. She tended to forget that he was old and his knees were, no doubt, a little creaky. "Come on in, I'm so looking forward to a break and Sarah was cooking chocolate cake. Her chocolate cake is enough to make me smile."

Amos turned and began to walk away. Ester knew she had to follow him, maybe she could do this. Such a greeting was friendlier than she could have hoped for. Amos understood everyone, maybe he would understand and help her.

Once they were sitting at the Beilers' table and eating cake with coffee, Ester let out a sigh.

"Was this just a social call, or is there something I can do for you?" Amos asked.

Ester felt unable to talk and she took another bite of the moist and delicious cake. Unfortunately, it seemed to clog her throat and she thought that she would choke.

"I can leave you to it," Sarah said.

"*Nee*," Ester managed. "It is not private and I would like to ask for both of your help."

"It is something we would be delighted to give," Sarah said as Amos pulled on his long grey beard and nodded his head.

Ester knew that she had made the first move, nothing had happened so she would make another. "I am working with Jeremiah Phillips, I do not wish to talk out of turn, we have discussed this..." The words froze in her throat once more. She had not discussed it in this much detail. Could she tell the Beilers that Jeremiah was struggling?

"Let me put your mind at ease," Amos said. "I know of their financial trouble. Henry and I had discussed it. He believed that Jeremiah would be able to turn things around, but, he asked that I be there if help was needed."

Ester let out a sigh. She should have expected this. Amos knew everything and was always ready to step in when his help was required. Suddenly, it came to her, he was there for her too. If she needed it, Amos and Sarah would always help her. Tears flooded her eyes and she wiped at them. "*Ack*, I'm sorry."

Sarah handed her a handkerchief and squeezed her hand. "Do not be. You have been through so much. We are here."

Ester patted at her tears and took a sip of coffee. Taking a breath she raised her head and told them of her idea. Of how she hoped that the district would all help and that they could turn around the fortunes of the brothers' farm. She did not mention her own need. It already seemed to have been met and she did not wish to appear selfish.

Amos clapped his hands. "That is a wonderful idea. I remember the time before. It was amazing."

"I just need to know how to do this," Ester said.

Amos was leaning forward and had picked up a pad and pencil. "There will be much to do and we want to do it as quickly as possible. I think maybe in two weeks, the Saturday before the following service."

Ester felt her mouth fall open.

"Do not worry, child, many hands make light work," Sarah said. "Now, I will make a new pot of coffee while you two brainstorm some ideas."

Amos chuckled. "We will need to advertise this and get the district involved. I can do the latter this Sunday at service."

"Maybe, it would be better if you don't tell them I'm involved," Ester said.

"Why ever would you say that?" Amos asked.

Ester shrugged. "It is not a secret that I'm unpopular. I would hate to spoil this for Jeremiah."

Ester felt a shock go through her, she could see a touch of anger on Bishop Amos's face. She had never seen him like that before. Of course, she had done the wrong thing again. She had ruined things, why hadn't she left this to Jeremiah?

CHAPTER SIXTEEN

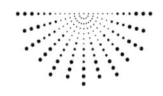

"I'm so sorry," Ester said as she stood, almost knocking the chair over.

"Please, sit." The anger had gone and Amos pointed back at the chair.

"I didn't mean to upset you. I am wrong. I seem to upset everyone, every time I speak. I know I should keep quiet and to myself."

"You did not upset me, I was upset at myself for not spotting this. You do not upset everyone and if you do upset someone, that is their problem, not yours." He took a sip of his own coffee and pointed at Ester's cup.

For a moment, she hovered. Half of her wanted to run home and shut the door. To lean against it and never come out again but another part needed to learn to negotiate the world without Aunt Rhonda.

"*Gott* loves you, do you believe that?" Amos asked.

"*Jah*," she managed but did she?

"Trust me, child. Genesis 1:27, So *Gott* created mankind in his own image,

in the image of *Gott* he created them; male and female he created them. If this is the case then how can you be wrong?"

Amos smiled and she felt better. "I... I... I don't know."

"You can't, you are perfect and we love you. Many people love you and respect you. I do not doubt that you have things to learn, we all have. That is our path but never think that you are not a valuable member of this district."

"*Denke*," she managed and had to wipe away a few more tears.

"I believe that your quilts are selling very well, is that right?"

Ester smiled and nodded. "I have made enough money for the whole year, more than we had ever made. Jeremiah persuaded me to join with him and I cannot *denke* him enough."

"Then you do not need this event to help yourself?"

"*Nee*, I prayed and the idea just came to me."

Amos nodded. "See, what a *gut* person you are. You need to let others see that light that shines from you."

"But I say the wrong things."

Amos chuckled. "Don't we all at times? You will learn, the first lesson is not to worry. If you upset someone don't take it personally, just tell them what you have told me and they will understand. We are going to turn the fortunes of the Phillips brothers around, I promise."

"I will talk about the event this Sunday at service. I will ask people to do as they did for the Mullet farm but before then we need to get this advertised in Bird-in-Hand."

"How?" Ester felt her heart pound and knew that her eyes were wide and her mouth open. This was happening so fast.

"That is easy. You go to speak to Stephen Fischer, tell him I sent you and that you need 500 flyers for the event. Tell him that I have asked for them out of the district fund."

"Can I do this? What will I put on them? What will I do with them?"

"You can do this. Stephen is a *gut* man, do not worry about what you say. Explain that you are helping a friend and he will know what to do. Once you have them, you and Leah can distribute them in Bird-in-Hand."

"Maybe, you or Jeremiah should do this?"

"Have confidence, He made you in His image." Amos winked.

"I will do my best."

"That is all I ask. Once you have done that there are two other people I would like you to talk to. Rachel King will be able to provide more quilts. The number of people we hope to get, you will not keep up. I realize that this will reduce your business, are you all right with that?"

Ester laughed. "It will take me some time to make more quilts, they are selling as fast as I can make them so I do not think I need to worry."

"That is as I thought. The next call you should make is the Millers' bakery. Other bakers can help, but the Millers are the oldest and most established. They will be able to help you out and they are very friendly."

"It is some time since I have visited the bakery. There was never a need. I could cook all that was needed and I hated leaving Aunt Rhonda alone too long."

"They will understand that, I assure you they will help. Just remember to have confidence in who *Gott* made you."

"But what if I do it wrong?"

"I remember someone saying to me that they fake it until they make it. I really liked that phrase. Remember Rhonda and think about how she would talk to people, see if you can be like her if you get stuck. You can fake it until you have more confidence, trust me that confidence will come. You have a bright future, I can see it now.

Fake it until you make it. Ester liked the sound of that, could she do it? Then it came to her, that she was not doing this for herself. She was doing it for Jeremiah and his brothers. She could do it for them, for him.

CHAPTER SEVENTEEN

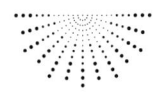

*E*ster decided that she would walk straight to the printer's shop. It was on the outskirts of Faith's Creek's main street. A business that she had seen but never entered. If she walked along the creek she would be there in a little over 20 minutes.

That would give her time to pray for guidance and to try to work out what to say. Amos had told her not to overthink things, but that was easier said than done.

The more she walked the more worried she became, maybe she should go to speak to Jeremiah and get him to do this. The thought made her smile and it calmed her. *Nee*, he was busy, she could do this for him.

The shop was up ahead. As she walked closer, a few people said hello and gave their commiserations. Ester found she was answering them easily, not thinking about it and they seemed happy to talk to her. But now, here she was and she froze outside the door. What if she messed this up, would it ruin Jeremiah's chances?

It didn't matter, she could not let the bishop down. Taking a breath she opened the door and walked in. It was a dusty place piled high with boxes and boxes, some overflowing with paper. There was a counter directly in front of her and behind it a big machine that a thin, stooped, grey-haired man was working on.

"I'll be with you in a minute," he said without looking up. He was pulling a handle and the machine made a great noise and paper shot out of one end. "There, all finished."

He turned and smiled, pushing thin round glasses up his nose. "How can I help you?"

"I... errr... I... well..." What was wrong with her, she couldn't get the words out. She wanted to tell him that she might be awkward, that the bishop had sent her, that she was trying to help Jeremiah but all that came out was a croak.

"Are you all right?" he asked, coming around the counter and pushing his glasses back up his nose. "Here, sit." He cleared some boxes off a chair and helped her to it. "Would you like a coffee or a glass of water?"

"*Nee*," she managed. Why was he being so nice when she was making such a fool of herself? "I'm sorry, Bishop Amos asked me to call in." That was it, that was all she could manage.

"That is *gut*, how is he?"

"Oh, he is fine. I... I..." By now Ester had expected the man to be angry and to tell her to spit it out. That is what used to happen at school but he didn't. Instead, he smiled and was patient and it freed her voice.

"I'm helping a neighbor, the Phillips brothers. Along with the bishop we are going to run an event, like the one at the Mullet's Farm."

"Oh, that was wonderful, what a great idea. You need me to do you some flyers?"

"*Jah*..." Her nerves had almost gone but then she remembered that the bishop had offered to do them out of the district fund, could she accept that?

"I know just what to do. Here, let me show you." He grabbed a piece of paper and some pencils and began drawing. He soon had a wonderful flyer, with everything on it that she could envisage. "We just need a date."

"Amos suggested not this Saturday but the one before the next service. Is that too soon?"

"Amos certainly knows how to get things moving. *Nee*, I can have these done for you by tomorrow. I imagine he told you to get me to use the district funds for this?" He pushed his glasses back again and smiled.

"*Jah*, he did. Is that all right?"

"*Nee*." He was smiling but she felt her stomach tumble. "I think this is a *gut* cause. It will be my gift to the event. Are you happy with this?" He held up the poster, leaflet, whatever it was to be and she couldn't help but smile.

"It is amazing. I didn't think I could do this."

"Of course, you can. You looked after Rhonda so well, you can do anything. Now, I will drop these off to you... or the Phillips? Once they are done."

"To me is fine, or I can come and pick them up."

"*Nee*, I will run them over. Have a *gut* day."

"You too." Ester left the shop amazed that she could do this. That despite her stutter and rambling she had sorted this out.

As she left the shop her elation left her. There were still two people to see and she wasn't sure if to go straight to them or if to go see Jeremiah. Now she wished she had brought the buggy. It was a long walk to go to the Millers' or Rachel King's and if she wanted to go see Jeremiah as well she would be walking for hours.

Then it hit her, what had she done?

Now, she had to let Jeremiah know that the event was in a little over 2 weeks. Would it be enough time, would he be angry with her for arranging the date without discussing it with him first?

CHAPTER EIGHTEEN

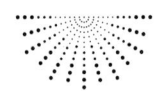

*E*ster felt drained, she felt as if she had let Jeremiah down. As if she had stolen his control and committed a sin. It was no *gut,* she had to go see him and admit what she had done.

Turning, she began the walk back. It didn't take long to get to the bank of the creek. A gentle breeze teased a lock of hair that escaped her *kapp*. Pushing it back and tucking it in she began to pray. In her mind, she prayed about what Amos had said. She prayed that Jeremiah would not be angry, that he would smile at her, and that she could help him and his brothers keep the farm.

The journey took no time at all, and by the time she arrived alongside their field, she was feeling much better.

Abraham and Moses were picking strawberries in the field nearest to the creek. Jeremiah was in the next field harvesting the tomatoes.

The brothers did not see her and she felt her confidence wane. They were working so hard and all she had done was conspire behind their backs. A flush of shame spread across her cheeks.

"Ester," Jeremiah called. "How are you this fine day?"

Ester looked up to see him walking toward her.

"We should keep working," Abraham called. "These crops won't pick themselves."

Jeremiah laughed and slapped his brother's back as he walked past. "Stand straight for a few minutes, it won't hurt you.

Abraham scowled as Jeremiah walked past but Moses stood upright, taking off his hat, wiping his brow, and stretching.

"*Gut* day," Jeremiah said as he stood in front of Ester with his felt hat in his hand.

"I spoke to Amos about the event," Ester said. "Why don't I help while we talk?"

"It's time for a break," Moses called. "I'll fetch some coffee down and cake. Would you join us, Ester?"

Ester gasped and nodded. A smile seemed to spread over her face of its own accord. Moses had asked her to join them. She couldn't remember anyone inviting her for coffee in a long time.

"Come, let's sit." Jeremiah guided her to the river bank where they sat in the shade of a tree. "Did he like the idea?"

"I have done an awful thing," she said lowering her head and grasping her apron in her hands.

"*Nee*, I doubt that. Tell me," he coaxed."

"Amos thought it was a great idea and he set things in motion. The event is to be held the Saturday before... not this service, but the next one."

There was silence between them and Ester held her breath. She had done the wrong thing. Slowly, she looked up to see a huge smile on Jeremiah's face.

"You are amazing," he said.

"I didn't mean to fix the date."

Jeremiah laughed. "Nothing stops Amos. What do we need to do?"

Ester explained and as she did, Moses and Abraham joined her. They asked questions, made suggestions, and planned as they ate pound cake and sipped coffee beneath the summer sun.

"How will we get the crops harvested in time?" Abraham barked. It seemed that he was determined to find fault with the plan.

Moses chuckled. "If Amos announces this at service, we will have all the volunteers we need. You know this, we have done the same for others."

"I guess," Abraham said. "I'm getting back to work." With this, he stood and wandered away.

"I'm sorry if I've caused any trouble between you," Ester said.

"*Nee*, you haven't," Jeremiah said.

"He's just grumpy, we know why, and he will get over it. I'm gonna get back to work too." Moses nodded, stood, and put on his hat before walking back to the field.

"Why don't I help you for a bit?" Ester said. "I can visit the other two tomorrow."

"I would love that." Jeremiah stood and offered her his hand to stand up.

Ester swallowed and took his hand. Once more a tingle went from his touch and left her breathless. She was no longer scared by the feeling but looking forward to it.

He handed her a box. "Have you ever picked tomatoes before?"

"*Jah*, we used to grow them."

"There are two sections in the box. The left for fruit that is ripe and needs eating quickly. That will be sold or bottled. We may dry some too. The right is for almost ripe fruit. This is what we will use over the next few days."

"How are you managing?" she asked as they worked along the rows. The work was hard but fun. Soon the box was heavy with tomatoes.

"We could do with some extra workers, but we can't afford to pay them."

Ester noticed that he had aged a little since Henry's death. The responsibility was like a heavy mantle on his shoulders. How she wished that she could ease that burden. But what could she do?

"You have been a big help, why don't you stay for a meal and I will run you home in the buggy?" Jeremiah asked.

Ester felt her heart stutter as she nodded her response. She knew that Aunt Rhonda would be so proud of her.

CHAPTER NINETEEN

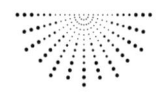

The meal was chicken and dumplings with buttermilk biscuits. Ester sat at the oak table in the surprisingly tidy kitchen while Jeremiah and Moses served the meal. Uri was sitting at the table and talking with his brothers. Abraham had not come into the room yet.

The brothers were excited about the open day, as they had decided to call it.

"I reckon we bottle as much as we can to sell, as well as the fresh fruit. What do you think? Can we get it all done? Uri asked.

"The district will help," Moses said. "I know I can sell bottled goods. My customers are already telling me what they would like me to stock. Milk, cheese, jelly, and chutneys are top of the list. Honey is also asked for on many an occasion."

"We could talk to Andy Lapp," Ester said and then felt fear freeze her heart as all eyes turned to her. Why had she interrupted them, why had she risked this? It had been so nice listening to them talk but now they would think she was interfering.

"Oh, *jah*," Moses said. "He sells all the honey products with... oh, now who did he marry?"

The two brothers shook their heads. "I don't know him," Uri said.

"I can't remember." Jeremiah shrugged as he pulled the tray of biscuits out of the oven.

"It was Rosella Esch; my friend, Leah knows them well," Ester said the words but they were spoken so quietly that she was surprised that they heard.

"Maybe, you could speak to her, get her to find out if they would like to sell from our stand." Uri's face was lit up with excitement, "or even get me an introduction. You are so helpful; we are lucky to have you as a friend".

"*Denke.*" Ester dropped her head for she knew that her cheeks were glowing with warmth. Was she really their friend? It felt right, it felt like a way forward.

"Abraham," Jeremiah called. "I'm dishing up."

Abraham came into the kitchen like a frosty breeze. It was as if he sucked out the joy and replaced it with worry. They prayed and then sat down for the meal.

Before they could eat much, Abraham stood up and picked up his plate. "I have a headache, I'll eat in my room."

As the door closed behind him Uri let out a sigh and Moses shook his head.

"I'm sorry if I caused trouble," Ester said.

"It is not you," Jeremiah said. "He is angry at me, he thinks I'm failing, but do not worry."

The mood lifted, and the brothers were all excited about the open day. Making so many plans that she knew they would not get them all completed but it was *gut* to see the fire in their eyes.

Ester relaxed as they ate the meal. The chicken was a little dry and the biscuits a little hard but Ester had never enjoyed a meal so much. All too soon it was over.

"I should go," she said standing. "I've enjoyed this so much, you must let me return the favor one day."

"We would like that," Jeremiah said.

"When it's my turn to cook," Moses said. "I can give you a list of dates." There was a grin on his face.

Ester felt as if she belonged, it was a strange feeling and it scared her a little.

"Let's get this open day over first," Jeremiah said. "You two can clean up while I take Ester home."

"There is no need," she said, and yet she wanted him to walk her.

"*Nee*, but it will get me out of the dishes." Jeremiah winked at her.

Ester felt as if warmth had seeded inside of her. It was wonderful and she knew she was grinning back at him.

"It won't take me long to harness a horse, you wait here."

"*Nee*, let's walk, it is not far along the river bank."

"It is a nice night." As he grabbed his hat he picked up a punnet and opened the door. "You two, get this tidied up, I won't be long."

Uri threw a towel at him, ducking as it came hurtling back.

Once the door had closed, Ester realized that it was dark. She had been here hours and yet the night had passed so quickly. Now, Jeremiah was walking her home, where was this going?"

"You have helped us so much, I thought you might like to take a few strawberries." Jeremiah waved the punnet.

"That is very kind, don't let me eat all of your profits."

He chuckled and began to walk. "A little thing like you, you look like you could do with eating a few *gut* meals."

Maybe she had lost weight. "Aunt Rhonda didn't have much of an appetite the last few months. I think I got so caught up in making sure she was happy, that I forgot to eat some days."

"*Jah, Daed* lost his appetite too. However, Moses," he chuckled, "he would never let me forget to make meals. He is like a bottomless pit."

They walked and picked strawberries and chatted. Ester found that it was easy and comfortable. She had relaxed so much that she was really enjoying herself. Part of her wondered if she could ever get this close to a man. Would it ever be possible for her to court?

It was something she had given very little thought to the last few years. Once Aunt Rhonda became more infirm there was no time to go to the night singing or to the games events. She had become a bit of a recluse. Doing so made her shyness even worse and she wondered if she had done the wrong thing.

Nee, she had done the only thing she could. Her time with Aunt Rhonda was treasured by her and she would never regret it.

Soon, they were back at her door.

"*Denke* so much for the meal and company," Ester said.

"It was my pleasure." He handed over the strawberries and his fingers touched her hand. Catching her breath she felt the flow of warmth tingle up her arm.

"I was wondering," he said as he clutched his hat before him. "I was wondering if I could drive you to service on Sunday?"

Ester drew in a breath and she must have looked shocked.

"I did not wish to insult you," he said. "If you wish, it can just be as friends. I... I want to say *denke* for all you have done."

Ester had a huge lump in her throat and her heart was pounding in her chest. Had he asked to court her or was this just an offer of friendship? It didn't matter, she would be over the moon at either. A smile spread across her face. "I would love that," she said.

Jeremiah smiled a huge smile that lit up his face to rival the moon. "Then I will pick you up Sunday. *Gut* night, Ester." Bowing, he put his hat back on his head, turned, and walked away.

Ester closed the door and leaned against it. Her heart was still racing and she was filled with joy. She had a friend; maybe, just maybe, she had the start of something more. "Aunt Rhonda, please don't let me mess this up."

CHAPTER TWENTY

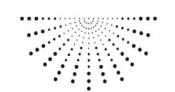

Saturday morning dawned bright and sunny. Ester checked on Ned and saw to his needs while a breakfast casserole heated in the oven. It was one she had made a few days ago and this would be the last portion. It always seemed to get better with time.

When she had eaten and finished her coffee she knew it was time to go and see the Millers or Rachel King. Why was she dreading it so much? So far, everything that Amos had asked her to do had turned out wonderful. She now felt as relaxed around the Phillips brothers as she had around Henry. Well, that was if she ignored Abraham's behavior. Something was definitely going on with him but she just didn't know what. A chuckle escaped her. Should she ignore the way Jeremiah made her feel? So alive, breathless, and excited.

After she had done the dishes she tidied the house, dusting here, sweeping there, and cleaning the surfaces. What was she doing? This was simply a form of procrastination, of putting off the tasks that needed doing. Aunt Rhonda would not be impressed.

Straightening her *kapp*, she grabbed a basket and set out on the walk to Faith's Creek. The Millers' bakery was the closest, but she decided to visit them second. That way, she could pick up some fresh bread and a few treats.

She knew very little of Rachel King. Of course, she had seen her at service and at other events, but she did not think that she had ever spoken to the woman. As she walked her nerves were making her feel weak and with every step, she wanted to turn and run in the other direction. What was wrong with her? Why was she so afraid?

Closing her eyes, she let her feet feel the ground and she began to pray. She prayed for the strength to help Jeremiah and for the strength to find new friends, and all too soon she arrived outside of Rachel King's house.

With her heart hammering, she walked up to the door and raised her hand to knock. The door was pulled open by a pretty little girl in a pink dress and a white *kapp*. "Hello," she said."

"I was wondering if Rachel King is here?" Ester asked.

"Who is it, Gloria?" A woman's voice asked.

"It's the shy woman." Gloria smiled and opened the door to let Ester in.

However, Ester's feet would not move. She was frozen to the spot, her heart pounding, her throat dry. Was that really how people saw her?

The door was pulled wide open by a woman who looked to be around 30. She had the pale skin of a blond with a splattering of freckles, she was a little plump but her smile was open and genuine. "Ester, it is lovely to see you, please do come in."

Ester tried to talk but nothing but a croak came out. Do what Aunt Rhonda would do, she told herself.

She was shown in and through a hallway and into a large and obviously working kitchen. The center of the room held the table, a large table made of oak. On it, were two plates with slices of cake a cup of coffee, and what looked like a glass of lemonade.

Behind it was an area dedicated to quilting, with a sofa, half-finished quilts, and a table with patches of material and thread.

"Take a seat, would you like coffee and some coffee cake?" Rachel asked.

Ester nodded and sat down. *What would Aunt Rhonda do?*

She was still finding it hard to speak and she didn't understand why this woman that she hardly knew simply invited her in and offered her refreshments. Aunt Rhonda would have understood though and she would have smiled and accepted such gracious hospitality. This should not have been a surprise, for it was the Amish way, however, Ester always expected to be shunned. Had she been wrong all this time? Had she made her own problems by being standoffish?

Soon there was cake and coffee in front of her and Rachel sat back down. "How can I help you?" Rachel asked.

Ester took a sip of the coffee and steeled herself to speak. Why was it so hard? Perhaps she worried that this woman would see her as a threat; after all, she was making her own quilts, and on the other side of the table there was a sofa in an alcove near the stove. It had at least three quilts on it in progress.

As she tried to talk again nothing but a croak came out. "I'm so sorry," she managed, "I'm not good with people." Then she felt Aunt Rhonda's presence and was filled with warmth; she could do this.

Rachel reached across and took her hand. "Do not worry, we are all friends here, take your time and tell me what you need." Rachel then turned to Gloria. "Why don't you go out and play in the garden?"

Gloria smiled and picking up her lemonade, she almost ran from the room.

"They have so much energy at that age, I wish I had it still." Rachel chuckled. "Now, I do not bite, talk to me."

Ester explained about the open day and that Amos had asked that she come to see if Rachel would like to sell quilts at it.

"That seems like a great idea, I would love to. How many would you like me to bring?"

Ester felt as if she was drowning. She had no idea how many to bring; everything was too much for her. Tears escaped her eyes and ran down her face. All she wanted to do was run home, lock herself in her room, and never come out again.

"Do not worry," Rachel said as she reached across and took Ester's hand once more. "I have been where you have. I do understand your grief, I also understand that you are almost in another world. You did so much for Rhonda, but over the last few years, you became a bit of a recluse. This must be hard for you, but do not worry, we are all here for you and you will be fine."

"I cannot *denke* you enough," Ester said. "I was worried, Jeremiah has been selling some of my quilts... I did not wish you to think that I was trying to steal your business."

"Never worry about such things. *Gott*, in His wisdom, would never let there be a shortage of customers. You have yours, I will have mine and there are many more for everyone else who sells quilts. I will bring as many as I can spare, and I will give 30% of the income to the farm."

"That is too generous," Ester said. "The brothers are not expecting this, they just want people to visit the farm and to buy their produce."

"I understand, but this is our way. I can afford to give and I want to. *Gott* has been gracious to me, I can be gracious to."

"*Denke.*"

"It is my pleasure, you must call in for a coffee sometime soon. We could talk and even quilt together if you wish to."

"I would love that," Ester said.

Soon she was on her way to the Miller's bakery. So far she had managed everything that Amos had asked her to do and she had gained new friends in the process. Life felt *gut*. Now all she had to do was talk to the Millers. Would her courage fail her or would she manage it?

CHAPTER TWENTY-ONE

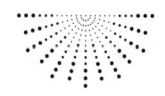

*E*ster made the walk from Rachel King's house to the Miller's bakery. It was famous in Faith's Creek and usually very busy. As she walked up to the door it opened and Mary Beachey came out with a big smile on her face. "*Gut* morning, Ester how are you doing?"

"I'm fine, *denke*, Mary, *denke* for asking." Smiling back, Ester stepped through the door and was surprised to find the shop empty.

Standing behind the counter that was filled with bread, cakes, cookies and delightful goods was a young woman she didn't recognize. At the moment, the woman was twiddling with the ties on her *kapp* and hadn't spotted her coming in. She had a fresh face, a fair complexion, with big rosy lips and bright blue eyes. There was a smile on her face as if she had a secret.

Ester paused; for some reason, she did not want to disturb this girl. Maybe she should come back another time? After all, she had done so well and she was feeling nervous and a little hungry. It would be awful if low blood sugar had her making a mistake and causing problems. Deciding it was the better thing to do, she turned and stepped toward the door.

"Oh, I'm sorry, was I ignoring you?" the voice came from behind her.

Ester turned around to see the young woman smiling at her and she shook her head. She couldn't really say that her nerves had given out and once again the words stuck in her throat. "I... I... I wanted to speak to one of the Millers. Bishop Amos sent me for a favor." The words had come out abrupt and the young woman's smile had slipped.

"My name is Hope Miller, it's my first day working here with no one with me. Have I done something wrong?"

"Oh, *nee,* it is me that is doing things wrong again. I just don't know how to talk to people. I'm sorry and the words are coming out all wrong." Ester knew that she was being rude and she wasn't meaning to so she took a big deep breath closed her eyes and let it out slowly. *Be like Aunt Rhonda!* Opening her eyes she tried to smile and hoped it wasn't too much of a grimace.

Hope ducked under the counter and came around. She pointed Ester to a table in the corner. "Do not worry, you are not getting things wrong. I remember the first day I served in the shop." She let out a little chuckle. "I think I dropped more of the cakes than I served. The more I dropped. the more flustered I became, the more I dropped. My *mamm* is Anna Miller, she just took me to one side and said, 'don't worry, you will get it'. I did, eventually." Another chuckle. "I'm not sure how much of the profits ended up on the floor though."

Ester smiled, Hope's enthusiasm was contagious as was her smile. "*Denke*, for being so kind."

"Would you like a cup of coffee and some chocolate cookies? They have just come through from the oven. They are so delicious when they are still warm."

"I wouldn't want to waste your time." Ester said.

"I can service if somebody comes in, and my feet are killing me. Let's have a break and you can tell me what you need." Without waiting for an answer Hope popped back under the counter and busied herself preparing 2 cups of coffee and two plates with two cookies on each.

She ducked under the counter again with a big smile on her face and put the plates and cups on the table. "Enjoy."

Ester sipped at the coffee and munched on the cookies. They truly were melt-in-the-mouth delicious. The chocolate hadn't even fully set.

"Now, how can I help you?" Hope asked, her eyes were bright and eager to listen.

"The bishop wants you to cater for an event at the Phillips farm," the words rushed out of Ester abruptly. "I'm sorry, what I'm trying to say is that the Phillips brothers are hoping to get a lot of people coming to the farm on Saturday the 20th. The bishop's idea was that they did an event a little bit like what happened at the Mullets' farm, sorry, but that might have been before your time." Ester was breathing heavily she was really making a mess of this.

"*Jah*, my *mamm* told me about that. I'm not sure whether you've heard about what happened when I was born?"

Ester shook her head, she hadn't.

"Well, my *dawdy* had gotten into a little bit of debt and my parents were going to lose everything. The whole district came together, they gave a little, and it added up to a lot, and saved our family. I know that they will want to help you. I think the best thing to do would be for us to have a stall selling refreshments, teas, coffees, lemonade and cakes, bread, and cookies. I'm sure that they will give some of the profits to the Phillips brothers. Would that be acceptable?"

"That would be wonderful, I can't imagine anything better," Ester said breathing a big sigh of relief but then it came to her this girl could only be 15. Did she have the right to agree to this?

The worry must have shown on her face because Hope raised her hands to her face covering her mouth and shaking her head. "Do not worry, I know that my parents will want to do this, I will get them to come and talk to you or to the Phillips, which would be easier?"

Ester wanted to do it herself but her nerves were shattered and she could not. Also, Jeremiah and Uri would be much better to decide where to put things and when they were needed. "*Denke, denke* so much. It might be better to talk to Jeremiah or Uri as they would have a much better idea of logistics than myself. They can, of course, talk to me, anytime they want to and please let them know I am very very grateful."

"That is *nee* problem, why don't I pack up a couple of those cookies for you to take home? They are on the house." Hope was already back under the counter and packing some of them into a bag.

"I couldn't accept them," Ester said. "You have already been so generous and you are doing an amazing job here. You are so friendly and so welcoming, I cannot say *denke* enough."

"I am always here if you ever want to talk to somebody. I would like it if you would be one of my friends."

"*Denke,* and if you ever need anything call on me, friend." Ester smiled as she took the bag and waved goodbye. Today had turned out to be a *gut* day. Tomorrow was Sunday and the way things were going she felt so optimistic about service.

It was the first time she had ever been driven to service and part of her couldn't wait whereas another part of her was terrified. It didn't matter, she was coping, she was imagining herself as Aunt Rhonda, she was getting through all of this. Maybe her life was about to get even better.

CHAPTER TWENTY-TWO

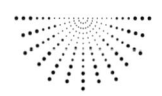

It was Sunday morning, and Ester paced around the kitchen. For some reason, her *kapp* wouldn't seem to stay where she put it. It felt as if it was constantly slipping and she would try and adjust it, only to find it was where it should be. Why was she struggling with this now? She felt like a *kinner* who was just learning to wear the prayer covering.

The sound of a horse on the road outside, brought her to the window, again. The buggy drove straight past and as it did, acid seemed to burn in her stomach. She had been too nauseous to eat this morning which was just not like her. *What if he doesn't come?* That thought had been going through her mind all morning. It was silly really. If

Jeremiah hadn't planned to pick her up and drive her to service, then why would he have asked her?

More acid seared in her stomach. Surely, he wouldn't be so cruel? She didn't deserve this, did she?

Glancing at the clock, she realized it was still early. That she was panicking for nothing. It was time to do something, at least that would salve her nerves. Pouring a cup of coffee, she buttered two rounds of bread and sat at the table. Though the bread was light and delicious it clogged her throat and she had to force it down. Still, she was going to do so. If and when Jeremiah turned up, the last thing she needed was for her stomach to rumble all the way to service.

When she had finished the bread she said a little prayer. It calmed her mind and made her realize that she was being silly. Whatever happened would happen and she would cope with it.

As she said amen, she heard another horse only this time she refused to jump up and run to the window. The horse got closer and closer and then she could hear the buggy turning around in her small front yard. He was here.

Ester grabbed her cloak and left the house to find Jeremiah walking toward her.

"*Gut* morning," he said with a huge smile on his face.

"*Gut* morning," she managed in reply and gave him a smile that she hoped wasn't too weak.

He offered her his hand to help her into the buggy and she tensed, hoping for that tingle that his touch always brought. She was not disappointed and she knew that her cheeks were glowing as she climbed into the buggy.

Jeremiah came around and climbed in beside her. "I'm sorry if I'm a little bit late, Abraham... well, he was being a little difficult this morning."

"Does he dislike me?" she asked.

Jeremiah let out a sigh and shook his head. "It is not you that he dislikes it is me."

"I cannot believe that. You are doing such an amazing job at such a trying time. Maybe he is still grieving?"

Jeremiah turned the buggy down the lane that led to the Lapp's farm which was there this fortnight's service was held. "I am trying my best. Before he died, my *daed*, Henry told me about the problems the farm had. Of course, I knew about them to some extent, but not quite how bad things are. He also asked me to make sure that the farm and my brothers were looked after. I wanted to keep that burden from them, as much as I can, is that wrong?"

"*Nee*, not at all. Does Abraham feel that it should be him making the decisions?"

"*Nee,* he thinks it should be Colin, my brother who left on *rumspringa* and didn't come back. One thing I haven't told my brothers is that my *daed*, Henry asked that I look after all of them and that included Colin. Maybe I have let him down, for so far, I haven't even tried to contact Colin. He asked me to do something else but I can't even mention that just now."

"Do not beat yourself up over this. Henry gave you three jobs to do and I am intrigued to know what the third one was." She chuckled a little when he gave her a look of horror. "You may keep your secret for now. Just remember, Henry gave you a great burden and you are tackling it in the order of priority. If you were to lose the farm there would be nowhere for Colin to come back to. Once we... apologies, I mean you, have some stability, then you can tackle the other tasks. That is the way Henry would have wanted it and your brothers will understand that in time."

"How did you get to be so clever?" He winked.

Ester chuckled and bowed her head. How could something so simple as a wink make her feel so alive? What was happening to her?

They had arrived at the Lapp farm and the conversation stopped while Jeremiah pulled the buggy in alongside all the others. Soon he was helping her down and Ester said her goodbyes and wandered into the service to find Leah.

"How was the journey?" Leah asked, her face lit up with a bright smile.

"It was *gut*," Ester said, knowing she was blushing.

"You two make a fabulous couple." Leah grinned as Bishop Beiler walked to the front of the barn to start the service.

The service was inspiring as always. In it, Amos talked of helping others. He mentioned the open day and asked that all who were willing to help make themselves known after the service. He finished it with a quote from

Hebrews 13:16. *And do not forget to do good and to share with others, for with such sacrifices God is pleased.*

As they walked out of the barn, Ester could see that people were already crowding around the bishop offering their support. But to one side, Abraham looked angry, his icy blue eyes were cold and distant. Jeremiah was trying to move away from the crowd to keep their conversation private, but it was to no avail.

"You are shameless, getting the bishop to beg for help," Abraham said.

"I am not, this is our way and this is how we serve others. Is it not written, *Ask and it will be given to you; seek and you will find; knock and the door will be opened to you*?"

"*Daed* would be ashamed of you, you are letting the farm fall into ruin and we will end up with nothing, all because you want to run around after that girl." With that, Abraham turned and walked off.

Ester felt tears running down her face. She knew it was her fault and she hated the fact that she had split the brothers up and that she had caused so much trouble. She should have kept to herself, but instead, she had caused this terrible strife.

She would not see Jeremiah again, she would not be a thorn between the two brothers. With her heart breaking, she looked at Leah. "Tell Jeremiah I've gone home and not to trouble me again. Tell him I'm sorry." With that, she turned, picked up her skirts, and ran.

"Ester, come back," Leah shouted, but it was too late for Ester had gone.

CHAPTER TWENTY-THREE

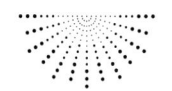

"I cannot say *denke* enough," Jeremiah said to James Yoder who had offered not only to provide a number of bottles and jars but that his family would help bottle the fruit.

Jeremiah had been overwhelmed by the outpouring of support from the district. He knew he should've expected it, knew he should've asked for it himself, but it had taken Ester to do this for him. That was when he realized that he was falling for her and falling for her fast.

At one time, he had thought her awkward and rude, though he had always considered her pretty. *Daed* had often spoken of her and her potential but Jeremiah had never seen it. Not until now. Suddenly, he wanted to share the good news with her and he turned around to see her almost running away.

There was something both proud and defeated in her stance. It was as if she was forcing herself to hold her head high, and yet, she had the world on her shoulders. What had happened? Then he spotted Abraham and anger burned through him.

Abraham was bitter, and he was taking it out on anyone. If he had taken it out on Ester then Jeremiah would be angry.

"Anger is not the way to solve this problem," Amos said.

Jeremiah looked up ashamed. "I know, but sometimes, Abraham drives me crazy.

"That is what brothers are for." Amos chuckled and pulled on his beard. "How are things going?"

"The support has been overwhelming and so generous. I feel like I ought to go after Ester, but it would be unfair when so many people wish to speak to me."

"That is what I thought," Amos said, "and why I called your brother over."

Jeremiah followed Amos's eyes to see Uri rushing over.

"Isn't this amazing?" Uri said a huge smile on his face. "I've got loads of things to put in the stall and sell and the generosity... the ideas, the help, it humbles me."

"It is *gut* to see you so happy," Amos said. "I need Jeremiah to run me an errand, could you take over organizing the open day?"

Uri's smile became so wide it nearly split his face and he was nodding with such enthusiasm that Jeremiah feared his head might drop off. "I would love to, I have so many ideas, so much I want to get organized. The stall is just so wonderful. I get to meet people, talk to them and I'm doing something I love. Yes, please, let me take over?" His eyes looked at Jeremiah asking for permission.

"I think you might be better at it than me, anyway," Jeremiah said, and the words rang true. Was he the right person to do this? Was he the right person to save the farm or should he move aside and let his brothers take over?

"Off you go then, Uri," Amos said and watched as he walked away.

"*Denke*," Jeremiah said and turned to go but Amos held his arm.

"I can see your doubts," Amos said. "A leader is not someone who is best at everything, he is someone who knows what he is *gut* at and what he needs to delegate. You are the right person to turn this farm around. You are the one that had saved it from going under up to now, at the same time as you looked after Henry. Have faith in yourself, you have done much more than the others."

Jeremiah was shaking his head. "My brothers have helped, it is not on me."

"*Jah*, they have, but you are the one who has been the solid ground to build the foundation on. Do not doubt yourself. Do not let Abraham cause you to falter. He's lost, but you will help him find what he needs. Trust in yourself."

Jeremiah knew that his cheeks were red for he could feel the heat almost glowing off them at such high praise. "*Denke*."

"It is my pleasure. Now, you should go after Ester. I fear your brother has hurt her. Let her know how you feel, but take it slowly, for her confidence needs building first." With that Amos released his arm.

Jeremiah nodded and ran to grab his horse. It would not take him long to put Copper back in the harness and he would soon catch up with Ester. If not, he would call on her at home. How he hoped that he was not too late and that he could undo any damage that Abraham had caused.

* * *

Ester brushed at her tears as she walked. She was angry to let them fall but she felt as if she had lost so much so suddenly. First, she had lost Aunt Rhonda, and with that, she had lost everything. Then she had prayed, and her prayers had been answered and she had developed this... friendship... or whatever it was Jeremiah. Her confidence had been growing in leaps and bounds and she thought the future was nothing but rosy... and yet, what Abraham said felt true.

She was trouble, and she was causing the brothers trouble, it was wrong to do that. The honorable thing to do was to let them go, to let Jeremiah go. That would hurt, but she would do it. She had survived before and she would survive again.

The sound of a horse and buggy coming up behind her made her step onto the verge. As she looked up she could see that it was Jeremiah. What was he doing? Why was he following her? Quickly, she wiped her tears and hoped that her eyes did not look too red.

The chestnut buggy horse pulled up alongside her and Jeremiah jumped down and came around to stand in front of her.

"I heard what Abraham said to you, and I am so sorry," he said.

"It does not matter, I do not wish to get between you."

"You haven't. I cannot say *denke* enough for all you have done for us and one day, Abraham will see that. Please, do not push me aside for I care for you and I want to keep seeing you."

Ester stared into his beautiful blue eyes and she could see that he was telling her the truth. She felt as if she could stare into those eyes forever, but she must not cause trouble for the brothers. "I don't think this is working," she said and even though it broke her heart she turned to walk away from him.

CHAPTER TWENTY-FOUR

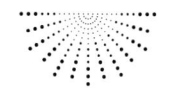

Ester had expected Jeremiah to get back in his buggy and go back to service. After all, the meal would be being served and it was a great social event that no one liked to miss. Sunday was the one day where they could all get together and talk and eat and relax and pray. Service was the one place where she always felt as if she was accepted, and today, Abraham had taken that from her.

With her head down she continued to walk, fighting back the tears, but to no avail. A hand touched her arm and she stopped and turned around. She was looking up into Jeremiah's eyes and when he saw her crying he pulled her into his arms and against his chest.

Ester knew that this was wrong, that she should not be held by a man, on her own, under such circumstances. However, she sank against his chest and felt safe in his arms as she let the tears fall. Would she ever feel safe at service again?

"It is all right," Jeremiah said as he stroked her back. "Abraham is not angry at you. I think he's really angry at himself and he is striking out at anyone to ease that pain. Please forgive him, and give him time to heal."

With her head on Jeremiah's chest, her tears soaking into his shirt, she felt safe and able to accept the words. She had always thought that other people were never scared like she was and yet... maybe they were. Maybe they were just better at hiding it than she was? If this was true, then nothing had changed.

Pulling back, she wiped her tears and looked up at Jeremiah. His face, his handsome face was full of concern and maybe something more. Did he care for her?

Ester swallowed. "I'm sorry I ran. I didn't want to come between you, but if what you say is true, then I can give him time."

"Then let me drive you home, or back to the Lapps', it is your choice."

"I would love it if you take me home," she said, and then she felt a surge of courage. "Perhaps, you would drive me to service, next time?"

"I would love nothing more. Maybe you could make me a coffee, for I would love to see some of the quilts you are working on."

"I think I can manage that, I might even be able to rustle up some fried chicken and potatoes."

Jeremiah smiled as he helped her up into the buggy. "You know the way to a man's heart."

Ester's own heart was beating so rapidly that she feared it would break from her chest and fly into the sky. How she hoped that his words were true.

CHAPTER TWENTY-FIVE

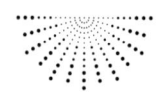

*E*ster and Leah worked late into the night. It was two days since the service and she had not seen Jeremiah since.

"My eyes grow weary," Leah said. "We need to add oil to the lantern or call it a day?"

Ester chuckled. "I can add some more oil. I wanted to get this quilt done."

"Might that be so that you can take it over to the Phillips' farm?" There was a strange look in Leah's eyes as if she knew something.

"Of course, I'm trying to help them as much as I can."

Leah chuckled and put down her quilt. "Enough, you do not need an excuse to go and see Jeremiah, I'm sure he will be delighted with a visit."

"Whatever do you mean?" Why was Ester denying her feelings? Was it because she was worried that it had all been a dream? *Jah*, he had driven her to service but everyone had seen her leave alone. What if he was only being nice, what if she was reading too much into this?"

"I mean, that he is very handsome," Leah said.

"Who?"

Leah laughed. "Jeremiah, of course. I can see how much he cares for you."

Ester felt her mouth drop open and she shook her head. "I... I don't think so."

"I do, let us have a mug of cocoa and talk for a while. We can let the flame burn low and it will help us get ready for sleep."

As they sipped at the cocoa, Ester listened to Leah telling her that Jeremiah liked her. Could it be true? Her mind drifted back to the afternoon of the service. He had driven her home and come in for coffee and lunch.

While she prepared the food, he looked at the quilts. "These are so beautiful, so delicate and intricate. You have a great talent."

Ester blushed and put the food on the table. They ate and talked about the weather and the harvest. About the many people who had offered to help but then Jeremiah stopped. He shook his head and looked at her and she could see the pain in his eyes.

"I fear I'm failing," he said. "Bishop Amos tells me I'm not, but the farm is in a desperate situation and my brothers are unhappy. I fear that I'm letting my daed down and that I might be best to let others take over. Maybe, someone who has been out into the Englischer world would have more ideas. Maybe, I should move over and let others take the reins."

Ester reached across the table and took his hand. She had experience with such feelings and she knew how Aunt Rhonda had spoken to her when she had them. Now she was going to fake it until she made it, she was going to use that knowledge to help Jeremiah.

"I do not think you are failing, I believe that Henry would be proud of you. You have to be patient; so far, you are sowing the seeds. They need time to germinate and grow before you can reap the harvest."

Jeremiah looked a little happier but then his face fell again. "What if I don't have time? Maybe, we shouldn't see each other, maybe I would be better focusing on the farm instead of wasting time."

"If that is what you want," Ester said, feeling deeply hurt that he thought she was a waste of time.

"It isn't. I'm so sorry I want to spend time with you but I want to make sure that my family can keep the farm."

Ester reached over and squeezed his hand. "We are going to make this work, just pray, work together and have faith."

"Ester, Ester, wakey wakey," Leah said.

"I'm sorry, I had drifted a little."

"I think you are very sweet on Jeremiah. I think it is a *gut* thing."

Ester smiled, she thought she was too, she hoped that he had not changed his mind.

* * *

It was the day of the open event and Ester and Leah arrived early at the Phillips' farm. Uri was the first one to greet them. "*Gut* morning. I have a place set up for you, right of the entrance," he said and pointed to the large table that was covered with a white cloth and had two chairs behind it. "If you need any help, shout to me, a few of the district have already started to arrive."

"We will be fine," Leah said. "He seems so excited," she said after he had walked away.

"I think he loves dealing with the customers." Ester felt full of enthusiasm and energy as she unloaded the quilts. Soon, the stall was set up and many of their other neighbors had set up similarly. The one next to theirs was Rachel King's, it was also piled high with quilts. There was furniture, bird boxes, all sorts of crafts, and cakes.

Ester was surprised to see that the brothers had set their own fresh fruit and vegetable stalls up at the furthest distance. It was even a little way away from the others, almost as if it was an apology. When you looked around the yard, it was not in a place for natural foot traffic and she felt a little worried. Would people even see the stall where it was?

"Ester, it is so *gut* to see you," Jeremiah said as he came over with a big smile on his face. "You have done so much for us and I missed you over the last few days."

Ester blushed. "It is my pleasure and it is *gut* to see you too."

"It doesn't look like many people are coming," Abraham said his arms folded across his chest.

"Would you just grow up, Abraham," Leah said, giving the man a solid smirk. "Maybe you should help, instead of standing there looking so sour that even lemons would be ashamed."

Abraham raised his head and his mouth dropped open. It was clear he had not expected such comments but he did not seem able to find a suitable reply. Shaking his head he was about to walk off.

"Perhaps if you helped, you could reserve judgment until the end of the day," Leah said.

"I will," Abraham said before walking away.

Jeremiah silently whispered *denke* to Leah and gave her a nod of gratitude. Approaching Ester, he took her hands in his. "I think we are ready and I think I can hear people coming." He squeezed her hands and smiled and then walked to start to welcome the people to the farm.

Their neighbors turned up in great numbers, and each bought a little something and chatted, drinking coffee and eating cakes. Then the Englischer started to arrive.

"Oh, my, look at these marvelous quilts," a woman with long blond hair said. "I have enough to buy one, I wish I had brought more cash, look at this beautiful pink one. Is this one still for sale?" she asked.

"It is," Ester said. She had already sold two quilts and only had a few more left but as she had suspected, people were not finding the brothers' stall and so far they had sold little or nothing to anyone outside of the district.

Abraham walked up to them and looked at Leah. "I told you this would fail. My brother needs to stand aside and let someone else take over."

Ester hated the strife between the two brothers; she knew she had to do something, but what could she do? Would it be best if she pulled away, was she causing the trouble?

CHAPTER TWENTY-SIX

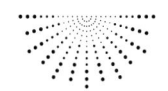

Then it came to her, they had everything the wrong way round. They should have placed the quilts as the last stall to see. Amish quilts were famous and many people had come just for them; however, given the choice they would buy much more.

"Excuse me," Ester said to the customer she was serving and she moved across to Leah. "Can you manage things for a few moments?"

"Of course."

"Leah will take care of you," she said to the woman. "I will be back in a moment."

Jeremiah was walking from stall to stall helping his neighbors and seeing that everything went smoothly.

However, the stress and worry were clear on his face. Everyone was selling something, everyone except the brothers.

As she approached, she noticed Abraham come up to him.

"Maybe you realize now that you're not up to this," Abraham said. "I think it's time that you stepped aside and let someone else take over the farm."

"The day is not over," Jeremiah said but it was clear that he was not expecting anything to save him.

"As I said, you need to step down and let someone else take over."

Before he could say anymore Leah appeared in front of him. The fury was clear on her face and she was pointing her finger straight at his chest. "Have you come across a new strain of corn or wheat or vegetable, something that turns into gold when it is planted?"

Abraham's mouth opened and closed but he said nothing.

"Then, maybe your time would be better spent helping, rather than pulling down everyone else's efforts. I am ashamed of you. Support your brother, and do your best to support the farm, rather than letting your childish anger spoil things for everyone."

With that, she turned and walked away.

Ester was shocked, she had never really been so angry. She certainly didn't know she had the courage to dress down someone as big and strong as Abraham. However, it gave her a moment to get Jeremiah away from his brother and she was going to take it

"Jeremiah, come with me," Ester said. Before waiting for him to acknowledge her, she wandered over to where Uri stood, despondent behind his stall.

"I have an idea," she said.

Uri tried to put on a smile but he was struggling. "It looks like people didn't come for strawberries and tomatoes."

"You brothers are too nice," she said. "Can you lift the stall?"

"*Nee*, it is too heavy," Uri said.

"Many hands make light work," Amos said coming up behind them. "I know exactly what you have in mind, Ester, you really are very clever." He turned to the men behind him. "Pick up the stall, and carry it so that it is the first thing that anyone has to walk past before they come to anything else."

"But that is not fair to my neighbors," Jeremiah said.

"It is very fair, they are here to help you and to support you. Let them." Amos chuckled. "We already moved Rachel's stall and Ester's along a little bit so that yours can go where hers was."

"I... I don't know what to say," Jeremiah said.

"I do," Uri said. "I have customers to serve." With that, he turned to the men and they all lifted the stall and began to carry it. It was a strange sight and a little bit awkward but once it was moved people naturally looked at the goods. There was so much there, eggs, strawberries, tomatoes, salad greens, cucumbers, and the bottled goods.

While the stall was set up, Abraham once more had words with his brother. Ester was not close enough to hear what was said but she saw Jeremiah walk away. There was defeat in the set of his shoulders and she wanted to run after him, but for now, she had to see that the event was a success. Once that was sorted, she would find him and find out why Abraham was so angry.

Soon, Uri was doing a roaring trade. Many of the people who bought products were asking about more. Some even asked about a regular box of certain items. Uri pulled out a notebook and began to take names and details of what people required. He was good at this, and on the spot, he could work out when they could supply it and how much to charge. Within an hour he had enough orders to keep the farm going for the foreseeable future. One of them was for a local store from Bird-in-Hand. It seemed, at last, that the brother's fortunes had turned around.

The event was going so well, everyone was praising the brothers' produce as well as the event. "Do you mind if I go find Jeremiah?" Ester asked Leah.

"*Nee*, you go. I think he went down to the river."

Ester had a sudden sense of worry. The event was a success, but had she lost Jeremiah in the process?

CHAPTER TWENTY-SEVEN

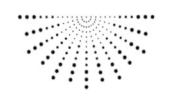

Jeremiah sat at the edge of the creek hating the fact that he had failed on all fronts. The event looked like it would be a disaster. Abraham was right, he was not fit to run the farm. He had failed his *daed*.

His thoughts went to his brother, Colin. The one who had left on *rumspringa* and never come back. The one he had not seen for so long. Colin had never committed to the church so he was not shunned. There was nothing to stop Jeremiah, or his brothers, from going to talk to him. So why hadn't they?

He knew in his mind, that he thought that Colin was simply playing at being an Englischer. That it was his own pride that had stopped him from coming home.

That pride had hurt their daed, but then, maybe there was fault on all sides. Henry had never visited Colin, and even though he had written, Henry had never replied.

Jeremiah put his head in his hands and prayed for guidance. Should he hand the farm over to Abraham? Should he find Colin and handed it over to him? Was it time to let the farm go? Deep in his heart, he knew that was not the case. Without the farm, what would they do?

The feel of a hand on his shoulder made him jump. He knew it was Ester, her touch was like the summer sun after a storm. It warmed him and gave him courage. "I'm sorry, I shouldn't have walked away but... well, if I didn't I might lose my temper. The problem is, I fear that Abraham may be right."

Ester came and sat next to him and reached out and took his hand. "I just came to tell you that Uri is doing a roaring trade. He has signed up many customers for the future and is supplying them with weekly boxes." Ester giggled.

Jeremiah realized it must be because of the look of shock on his face. "Weekly boxes?"

"I don't know, but Uri was so excited."

"You say it is a success?" Jeremiah could hardly believe the words. Was she just saying this to make him feel better? She didn't have to, just her presence made him feel better. Perhaps the doubt showed on his face.

"Believe me, the event is a success. Before the end of the day, you will have sold everything you have."

Jeremiah didn't quite know what to make of this. It was not his success, but Ester's and the districts. Even though he knew it should bolster his confidence, it didn't. He was failing. He closed his eyes and asked for guidance as to what to do. A light touch on his cheek was like the message he needed and he opened his eyes to look deep into hers.

"Smile, you're going to save your farm, you're going to keep your family together. Believe in yourself and have faith."

Jeremiah stood and walked away. "I wish I could believe in myself but I've done so much wrong. I have a brother, named Colin, he walked away from us and I have never been to see him. I have no relationship with my own brother, what sort of man does that make me? I upset you so much over Rhonda's funeral. I can never undo that."

Ester reached up and pulled him into her arms. For a moment he wanted to pull away, even though he didn't. He wanted to stay in her arms forever but he didn't think he was *gut* enough. He didn't think he deserved it.

"You need to give yourself time to heal," Ester whispered against his ear. "You have done nothing wrong to me or to anyone. Aunt Rhonda's funeral was simply a mix-up and she would understand, she would forgive as do I. You need to forgive yourself."

"I'm not sure if I can, I'm not sure how to start."

"Whenever I get stuck I asked *Gott* for help and then follow His guidance. Let us offer prayers for these recent events. You are a *gut* man, what would *Gott* have a *gut* man do?"

Jeremiah chuckled. "I think He would want me to stop sulking. I think He would want me to walk back over there and help with the sales. I think He would want me to reconnect with my brother, with two of my brothers. And I think He would approve of me having you in my life."

"I think He would want all of those things," she said looking up at him and hoping that her cheeks were not glowing too brightly.

They made their way back to see Uri surrounded by customers. He had already sold out of some items.

For the rest of the day, Jeremiah worked with his brothers and the rest of the district. He organized crews to go into the fields and harvest to keep up with the ever-increasing demand and he knew that he had a smile on his face.

The day flew past and soon it was over. Most of the neighbors and customers had left and there was just a little tidying up to do.

Jeremiah took Ester to one side and clasped her hands in his. "I cannot say *denke* enough. I want to continue working with you, to continue seeing you. Who knows what we may achieve if we work together."

"I would like that very much. Are you asking for simply a working relationship?"

"Hey, brother," Uri said. "We have done so well, I haven't added it all up yet but this will keep us going for months and I have orders to fulfill for weeks to come."

Jeremiah looked at Ester, he wanted to talk to her, he wanted to tell her that he wanted much more than just a working relationship with her, but it was not the time in front of his brother. This had to be done in private. "I will talk to you later," he whispered and hoped that the look on her face was not one of disappointment.

"The farm is saved," Moses said as he rushed over.

Was it really? Jeremiah hoped so. He noticed that Abraham stood to one side. There was still a scowl on his face, and as he watched, Leah walked past him and gave him a smirk. Abraham did not look too happy.

"I think we should all have a meal," Moses said. "To celebrate, and I don't know about you lot but I haven't had a chance to eat today and I'm starving. Apart from this, Mabel Glick left his wonderful-looking sausage casserole.

"That sounds like a great idea," Jeremiah said.

"We will leave you to it," Ester said.

"*Nee,* you two have been instrumental, you especially, Ester. It is only right that you have pride of place at our table," Moses said.

Jeremiah was so pleased that his brothers could see how much Ester had done. Hopefully, he would be able to drive her home after the meal and they could finally get a chance to talk. If he plucked up the courage to do so.

CHAPTER TWENTY-EIGHT

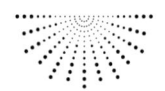

The sausage casserole was warming, filling, and delicious. Moses had placed it in the oven to reheat, along with some bread. Then he made coffee while they all sat around the table.

Everyone in the room was buzzing. The conversation was exciting and enthusiastic as they were all looking forward to the future, all except Abraham who sat quietly in the corner.

Ester noticed Leah looking at him every now and then. What was going on between the two of them?

Quite suddenly, the conversation stopped. It was dark and late and they were all tired.

"I have kept you too long," Jeremiah said. "Just give me a moment, and I will fetch a buggy and take you ladies home." With that, he left the room.

Abraham got up and left the room, without saying a thing.

Uri threw a dishcloth at the door he had just walked through. "What is wrong with him today?"

"Today." Moses chuckled. "He's been grumpy since we lost *Daed*."

"*Ack*, I should have given him more time," Uri said.

The buggy pulled up outside and Ester and Leah said their goodbyes, once again receiving much praise from the brothers.

"You are both, always welcome," Moses said.

"*Denke*, and *gut* night," Ester said. She wanted to ask Leah what was going on with her and Abraham, for she was sure that something was. "What is it with you and Abraham?"

"I just hate to see him behaving so badly," Leah said but before she could say anymore, Jeremiah was there to help them into the buggy. Ester wanted to push it, but it was too late to say much more and she did not wish to worry Jeremiah.

Jeremiah helped them in and then turned the buggy right out of his driveway. That was the way to Leah's house and even though it was further to her place than to Ester's, Ester was pleased he had done it this way around. She wanted to spend time alone with him and yet she was also terrified to do so. So much of their time together had been going into saving the farm. It felt as if that was done now, so what did they have left? Was it anything?

There was little conversation on the drive to Leah's. They were all tired, and good enough friends to not need it.

Jeremiah climbed down to help her out of the buggy.

"*Gut* night, see you soon," Ester called and she heard Jeremiah giving his *denke* once more.

Leah waved and walked into her home.

"How are you doing?" Ester asked as Jeremiah climbed back into the buggy.

"I am doing great, *denke* to you."

This time, the silence seemed oppressive. It was as if both of them wanted to talk, but neither of them could decide what to say. All too soon, the horse had stopped outside of Ester's home.

Jeremiah jumped down and was waiting for her by the time she opened the buggy door. He took her hand and the familiar tingle of excitement raced up her arm.

"Let me walk you to your door," he said.

"There really is no need."

"I wanted to talk to you. I'm sorry, sometimes I don't know what to say." They had stopped in front of her door and he shrugged. The gesture was clear in the moonlight.

"What is wrong?" she asked.

"There is something about you that has intrigued me from the start," he said. "Getting to know you better, I like you, I like working with you, I hope that we can be good friends like Henry and Rhonda were."

Ester felt her heart stutter. Was that all he wanted, friendship? Swallowing, she fought back her pride and knew that she had to push this. "Is that what you want? After all, Aunt Rhonda and Henry never courted or married, perhaps theirs was only a friendship and there is nothing wrong with that. Is that what you want, for us to stay in the same place, possibly marrying others and leaving our offspring to sort out similar matters in the future?"

The silence seemed to stretch before them and Ester felt the sting of tears in her eyes. She had let her heart escape her and fallen too quickly for it seemed that she was resigned to being nothing but the business partner.

"Ignore my words if they cut too close to your core," she said and reached up to open the door.

Jeremiah's hand on her arm sent shivers down her spine. Then he pulled her back to his side. Ester stared up into his eyes. "What are you thinking?"

She could see him swallowing in the moonlight as his Adam's apple bobbed in his throat.

"All I know is that I wish to keep seeing you," he said. "I want to get to know you better. I want to make up for the mistakes of my past. I want to drive you to service every fortnight. I want to work with you, *jah*, but I want more. I want to court you. Is that something you could cope with?

With a sigh, Ester relaxed into his arms. "I like the sound of this new plan. The idea of moving forward together seems like the answer to every one of my prayers."

Slowly, he moved toward her and their lips touched in the moonlight as he sealed the deal with a kiss.

EPILOGUE

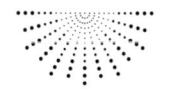

Over the next month, Jeremiah and Ester spent much time together. After the open day, the farm just got better and better. They had retained a number of loyal customers. More came each week to see Ester's quilts, and when Ester had sold out, they sold those of Rachel King's.

Three of the brothers were happy and content, though Abraham still moaned as much as he always had, and this was making Jeremiah sad.

One day, as they sat by the riverbank, eating fried chicken and drinking lemonade, Ester reached out to take Jeremiah's hand. "I see you are carrying the weight of the world on your shoulders, once more," she teased gently.

"I worry about Abraham. He will not open up to me about what is wrong. He no longer says that I am letting them down with the farm, but something is wrong. Don't get me wrong, there are days and times when I still grieve for my *daed*. There are times when the grief cuts me down like a knife to the gut. But I know this is not what *Daed* would want and I do not think it is the problem with Abraham, I just wish I knew what was."

Ester took his hand in hers. "I have days the same over Aunt Rhonda. I believe they are getting further and further between. Sometimes, I can even remember the good times without getting too sad. Have you any idea what is wrong with Abraham?"

"I wonder if it could be Colin. I sent him a letter, but I have not heard anything back. Maybe, it is time that I made the next move."

"I am here, if you wish me to come with you."

The smile that came over his face filled her with joy.

"I think I am ready to make the next move and on something else as well," he said and turned more to face her. Reaching out, he took both of her hands in his and stared deep into her eyes.

Ester felt her heart miss a beat. The touch of his hand still thrilled her as did looking into his eyes or seeing his smile. Part of her was terrified, this seemed too *gut* to be true, could it all end?

"Ester, I love you, and I want to ask you to be my *fraa*; will you marry me?"

Ester squealed with joy and leaped into his arms. She was placing tiny kisses on his face. "*Jah, jah*, I love you too and I can think of nothing better than being your *fraa*. *Jah*, I will marry you."

He held her in his arms and kissed her forehead. "I am so pleased to hear you say that, especially as I have already spoken to Bishop Amos. We have an appointment with him tomorrow and if you agreed, he's going to announce it at this week's service."

"That is *wunderbar* news. I can't wait."

Jeremiah moved so he was leaning back against a tree and pulled her to sit next to him. With his arm around her they relaxed in the sunshine and thought of the delightful future, they had together.

* * *

TWO MONTHS LATER

Ester was wearing a pale blue dress, very similar to her everyday dress, and yet very special. She had only just finished it the week before along with Leah's help.

It was Leah who was helping her into it now and making sure that her hair was neat and beneath her *kapp* and that everything was in place.

Ester felt special and proud and she knew that both were a sin, but somehow, she didn't think *Gott* would mind today. Though an Amish wedding dress was almost exactly the same as a normal everyday dress, Ester understood that every bride felt special.

"Are you nearly ready?" Leah asked. "They're all waiting for you downstairs."

They were in one of Bishop Beiler's spare bedrooms and Sarah had been helping them all morning. As Ester did not have family, the Beilers had offered to host the wedding. Ester couldn't think of a better place for it to happen but part of her wondered how many would turn out. No one had visited her home after Aunt Rhonda's funeral and she was well-liked by all in the district.

Traditionally, everyone who is available would come to a wedding. There was a great fear inside her, that no one would be there.

"Stop looking so worried," Leah said. "You are marrying a wonderful man who loves you dearly. I am very jealous." Ester chuckled and pushed her toward the door.

"I can't help it. I just remember how awful I was to him at the funeral. I'm so surprised that we ended up getting together. I don't know what happened to change things, but I expected us still to be at odds."

"Maybe it was *Gott* that saw how ideal the two of you are for each other. Maybe it was Henry or Rhonda. I do not know, but I do know that you are keeping people waiting, so, come on, let's go."

Leah pushed her out of the room to find Sarah on her way upstairs.

"How are you doing?" Sarah asked, the smile on her face was so welcoming that it eased Ester's nerves.

"I am fine."

Once they were all at the bottom of the stairs Leah took one arm and Sarah took the other and they led her to the barn.

As they walked across the ground to the entrance, Ester could see all the buggies from the district lined up, and all of the horses waiting in the paddock. Most of the people were inside, but some were still milling around and every one of them gave her a happy smile and congratulated her as she walked over.

As they entered the barn, she could see that it was full. It looked like everyone had turned up and was waiting to celebrate her marriage. For the first time, she didn't feel as if she had to run away. She felt accepted and wanted. It was a freeing feeling and she lifted her head a little higher and smiled a little brighter.

Standing at the front of the barn, in front of Bishop Beiler was Jeremiah. He looked so handsome in his suit and as she came in he turned and smiled at her. Ester felt as if she floated across the ground toward him, drawn by his love and his support.

Ester did not hear much of the wedding ceremony, it felt like but a blink of an eye before they were pronounced husband and *fraa,* and were walking back to their friends and neighbors.

"Give the happy couple a few minutes and let us set everything up," Sarah said as she shepherded people away from them to prepare the barn for the meal. She gave Ester a warm hug before leaving herself.

Jeremiah took her just behind the barn and pulled her into his arms. "You have made me the happiest man alive," he said before kissing her sweetly on the lips.

"You have saved me," she said before she kissed him back.

"With you by my side, I know I can do right by my *daed* and make my siblings happy, all of them. I no longer worry about the farm. As you said, break these things down into tasks and that one is solved."

"So what is the next task?" Ester asked.

Jeremiah chuckled. "My brothers would be horrified to hear, but *Daed* asked me to see them married... all of them, here on the farm and married. Do you feel up to the task?"

"I do, together we can achieve anything. However, I think if we make them happy, then marriage would take care of itself."

"You are so clever, my beautiful *fraa*." He kissed her once more. "We should go back inside, they will soon be missing us."

"Just a second," she said before she reached up and kissed him again, she was never going to get tired of this.

* * *

Leah wandered over to Abraham and smiled up at him. "What do you think of Jeremiah's plan now?" she asked.

"My brother seems so sure of what will happen next. I am not so sure."

Leah sighed, why was Abraham so grumpy? She began to walk away but he caught her arm and pulled her back. She gave him a look that made him drop her arm.

"I'm sorry, I didn't mean to startle you. I hope that you will keep quilting with Ester and that we will see you on the farm from time to time."

"I am loyal to Ester, of course, I will do so."

"Then I will enjoy your company at least."

He smiled at her and she turned and walked away. Maybe, she could get to know him a little better, maybe she could be the one to fill his heart.

As she walked outside to take a breath of air she noticed a man standing behind one of the buggies. What was he doing? He seemed to be hiding. As he peered around the vehicle she wondered if it was one of the Phillips brothers. He had red hair but he seemed older than Uri, closer to Jeremiah's age. Could this be Colin?

Deciding that she should go to say hello she stepped toward him. The man spotted her and disappeared behind the buggy and at the same time, Ester and Jeremiah walked up to her.

Ignoring the strange man she smiled at her friend. "Congratulations, you two."

Ester pulled her into a hug. "*Denke, denke* for everything, I could not have done it without you."

"I am starving," Jeremiah said, "let's go eat. We have the rest of our lives to be happy but my stomach is worried that I will not make it if I do not give it food soon."

Ester laughed. "*Ack*, I cannot lose you on my wedding day. What would Amos say if I let you starve?" She laughed with sheer joy. Taking Jeremiah's arm on her left and Leah's on her right, she marched into the barn and she realized that she belonged. That she had friends and that she was happy. The future was an adventure that she couldn't wait to experience.

* * *

If you enjoyed this book you can grab book 2 here

THE AMISH LANDSCAPE – PREVIEW

The wind lifted the ties of Emma's kapp and let them drift across her face. The breeze was nice, refreshing, and gave her a sense of freedom as did the open view before her. There was still a chill in the air and spring was yet to bring the hedges to life, but she loved this time of year.

Behind her was the center of Faith's Creek and she could still smell the enticing smells from the bakery. To her side was a cup of coffee and a raspberry and white chocolate muffin nibbled on but almost forgotten. In front of her was the widest part of the creek, or river, that the district was famous for. The sky above was blue, the blue so deep and perfect it made you feel small. It gave you a sense of the wonder of *Gott's* world, of the magnificence in the smallest things that could be taken for granted if you let them pass. The occasional cloud drifted across in front of her. They seemed lazy and indulgent, not quite as fluffy as the cumulus clouds of summer but still, they lifted her spirits. What would it be like to fly high like a cloud?

Emma chuckled, her sister Susan would consider such thoughts wasteful, "How will that get you a husband?" She could almost hear the stern tone in her voice. Lifting her paintbrush she let it slide across the paper and as if by magic the cloud was now immortalized in front of her.

Normally when she painted, she liked to work somewhere more remote. Tonight she only had time to walk here if she was to get any painting done. She had left her work in the clothing factory, ridden her bike back to Faith's Creek, and grabbed a sandwich and two muffins before sitting down to paint. Maybe two was too many, what would Susan say? That reminded her of the muffin and she lifted it and took a bite but her eyes were pulled back to the scene and how best to bring it to life on the paper before her.

The other side of the creek was pastureland and grazing on it were two large Belgian draft horses. The animals seemed to capture the sunlight and it enhanced the dapples on their chestnut coats and made their flaxen manes and tails shine.

It was Emma's second day on this painting and even though the horses had moved she had already penciled them in. All she needed to do now was capture the magnificence and the glory that embodied the horse's spirit. Holding her breath, she dipped her brush into the water and then back to the pallet, picking both orange and brown she mixed them together and delicately applied them to the paper. It was perfect, the brush glided from her hands bringing the horses to life.

Emma took another bite of the muffin as she studied the horses and their muscles. She had it, and still with the muffin in her left hand, she bent back to the painting.

Every now and then, she could hear voices behind her but one particular voice made her brush freeze above the paper. It was Amity Wayne. Emma bit back a groan. Amity was well known as a bitter old woman, a gossip, and someone who liked to pull others down.

"No wonder she's so fat," Amity said not caring that her voice carried.

Emma could not see who she was talking to and whoever it was, they were good enough to keep their reply to a whisper.

"Mark my words," Amity said again, "I don't think it's right. It goes against the Ordnung. I shall be talking to the bishop. Vanity and frivolity that's all it is, there should be no vanity in our district."

"I agree with you," another voice said.

The brush was shaking in Emma's hand. Yes, she was a little large, but surely that was the way *Gott* made her? It didn't matter. Cruel remarks had been part of her life for as long as she could remember. Emma Byler, 37 and still unmarried. 37 and hardly been courted. The woman could lose her home because she hadn't bothered to get a husband. The woman who wasted her time painting when there was work to be done. Who would even look at her! She had heard it all and even though she pretended she was strong, that she didn't care, it still cut her to the bone.

Biting back her tears she added more paint to her brush, but as she touched the paper her hand shook so badly that it smudged. The painting was ruined.

Rinsing her brush once more she wiped it clean and packed away her things. Luckily, her journey home would be in the opposite direction to Amity. Hopefully, they wouldn't meet.

With her paints, brushes, and easel all gathered under her arms, Emma started on her walk home. Even though she knew it was silly, she couldn't help but let a tear fall. Her work in the *Englischer* factory was hard, but it kept a roof over her head, just, and gave her enough money to spend on her painting supplies. Though there had always been a few mumblings about her paintings — until her *daed's* death — no one had said it out loud. Marlin Byler was a jolly man, even after his stroke. A good man who loved his community, but would not hear a bad word about his daughters.

Emma guessed that it was fine to have a little frivolity when you were looking after a dying relative. For a moment she was angry and feelings of pity overwhelmed her. Her sisters had it so easy. They were much younger than her and yet both were married. Susan had a three-year-old, little Dan. Mary had been married a few years now but so far had no children. Sometimes that worried Emma but her sister had not spoken about it.

Emma whispered a prayer of gratitude. Even though her *mamm* had been ill since Mary, her youngest sister, was born, they had had a good life. Emma had raised the two sisters and helped her *daed* as much as she could. It left little time to court and though she had always been happy, Emma had turned a little bit to food for comfort. Caring was hard work for a young girl and yet she wouldn't have missed it for the world. The hours she had with her *mamm* were treasured.

Emma walked past a large hedge up to a crossroads, struggling to carry all of her equipment and deep in thought. *What would she do if she lost her job?* Without looking she stepped out and was so engrossed that she didn't notice the buggy trotting towards her.

"Whoa!" A deep voice called.

The sound of hooves clattering to a halt sent a shock that jolted her heart and tingled all down her arms. Emma looked up to see the horse almost on top of her. She stepped aside quickly but dropped her easel and water-color pad onto the track. For one awful moment, she thought the horse and wheels of the buggy would go straight over it. However, the buggy was expertly steered around it and pulled to a halt.

Emma dropped to her knees to gather up her supplies. Could this day get any worse?

* * *

Jesse King looked out over the horse's ears as it trotted along the country lane. Faith's Creek was everything he could've hoped for and he knew that within a short time he would have more customers than he could manage. The local Bishop, Amos Beiler had invited him here as the previous blacksmith had retired. In his Ohio community, his brothers ran their family blacksmith and Jesse, even though welcome, had been looking for a new start. It was just a few years since his parents had passed, within a few months of each other. It seemed that their love was so strong that one could not survive without the other.

Shortly after that, the woman he had been courting had left him for a better prospect. It broke his heart and left him bitter and he had not approached a woman since. Although he knew that Rebecca's Zook did not deserve his love, she had it, and though he had now left her behind, his heart was still broken. It felt like a wizened old walnut to him. Hard and impenetrable.

It was at that time that he started to wonder about leaving his home. The memories were bad enough, seeing Rebecca married to Aaron Wagler was hard, but the hardest thing was the sympathy. Although he loved his aunts and uncles and brothers and their wives they were constantly plying him with sympathy. Either that or they were offering up alternatives. Jesse was not ready to give his heart again and he wondered if he ever would be.

Over the top of the hedge, he could see a young woman walking up to the crossroads. Her head was bowed and she seemed to be carrying a heavy load, both physically and metaphorically. As the horse approached the corner he waved to her but she did not look up. A hand clutched onto his heart as he realized she hadn't seen or heard him and she walked straight out almost under the horse's hooves.

"Whoa!" he shouted, hauling on the reins and steering the horse to the side. The woman raised her head and dropped all she was carrying. Jesse pulled the horse to a halt and jumped down. How could he have been so silly? He nearly ran her over!

The woman had dropped to her knees and was busily gathering up her things. Though she was dressed in the traditional Amish garb with a kapp, a dark blue dress, and a white apron. He could see that she had dropped what looked like art supplies.

The words of Bishop Bender were harsh in his ears. "Frivolity and wasteful time will not be tolerated. Work, young man, work and prayer, that is our way." He had heard them many times in his youth when he used to sketch. That was when he realized he hadn't picked up a pencil to do anything other than work in many years.

"Here, let me help you," he said bending to his knees.

She seemed oblivious and he reached out to grab her pallet of paints and at the same time she reached out too. Their hands touched and she turned to him and he saw the most beautiful pale blue eyes he had ever seen. There was something in them that pulled at his heart, was it the deep sadness, or was it something else?

Jesse felt his cheeks color and pulled his hand away as if it was burned. This was ridiculous. He was a man of 40. There was no way a woman should make him blush but there was something about her. She was beautiful and curvy with a face that looked worried and was damp with tears when he imagined it would bring out the sunshine if she smiled.

"I'm so sorry," he said. "Let me help you."

Of course, she must be married, she was beautiful and maybe a few years younger than him. Quickly he pushed away the feeling that this meeting was meant to be and tried to help. How would it look if the first week in his new district he upset one of its members?

She nodded her head and bowed so he could not see her face. Jesse wanted to comfort her but instead, he picked up her pad. It had opened to a watercolor of a small copse of trees not far from here. Cattle grazed in front of it and a bird sat on the hedge. It was so real, so beautiful that he wanted to touch it and he knew that his jaw had dropped open. "Did you paint this?" he asked.

The woman stood up and folded her arms. "I don't need you telling me I shouldn't be wasting my time," she said and grabbed the pad before turning and walking away, her arms overloaded.

Find out if Emma and Jesse can overcome their difficulties in The Amish Landscape.

ALSO BY SARAH MILLER

All my books are FREE on Kindle Unlimited

If you love Amish Romance, the sweet, clean stories of Sarah Miller receive free stories and join me for the latest news on upcoming books here

These are some of my reader favorites:

The Amish Faith and Family Collection

A New Amish Love

A Return to Faith

15 Tales of Amish Love and Grace

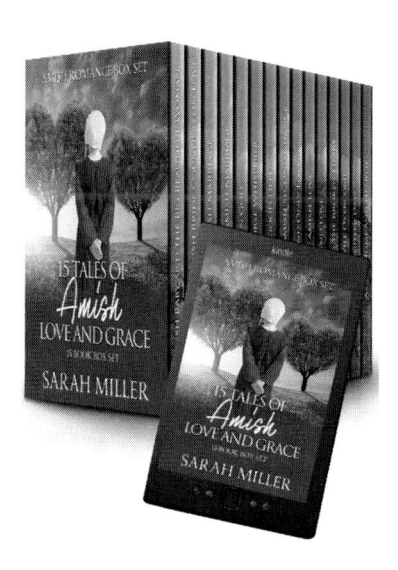

Find all Sarah's books on Amazon and click the yellow follow button

+ Follow

This book is dedicated to the wonderful Amish people and the faithful life that they live.

Go in peace, my friends.

As an independent author, Sarah relies on your support. If you enjoyed this book, please leave a review on Amazon or Goodreads.

ABOUT THE AUTHOR

Sarah Miller was born in Pennsylvania and spent her childhood close to the Amish people. Weekends were spent doing chores; quilting or eventually babysitting in the community. She grew up to love their culture and the simple lifestyle and had many Amish friends. The one thing that you can guarantee when you are near the Amish, Sarah believes is that you will feel close to God.

Many years later she married Martin who is the love of her life and moved to England. There she started to write stories about the Amish. Recently after a lot of persuasion from her best friend she has decided to publish her stories. They draw on inspiration from her relationship with the Amish and with God and she hopes you enjoy reading them as much as she did writing them. Many of the stories are based on true events but names have been changed and even though they are authentic at times artistic license has been used.

Sarah likes her stories simple and to hold a message and they help bring her closer to her faith. She currently lives in Yorkshire, England with her husband Martin and seven very spoiled chickens.

She would love to meet you on Facebook at https://www.facebook.com/SarahMillerBooks

Sarah hopes her stories will both entertain and inspire and she wishes that you go with God.

©Copyright 2022 Sarah Miller
All Rights Reserved
Sarah Miller

License Notes
This e-Book may not be resold. Your continued respect for author's rights is appreciated.

This story is a work of fiction; any resemblance to people is purely coincidence. All places, names, events, businesses, etc. are used in a fictional manner. All characters are from the imagination of the author.

Manufactured by Amazon.ca
Acheson, AB